The Essence of Love

by Zoe Burton

The Essence of Love

Zoe Burton
Published by Zoe Burton
© 2016 Zoe Burton

Early drafts of were written and posted on fan fiction forums in October of 2016.
ISBN-13: 978-1-953138-33-0

Acknowledgements

First, I thank Jesus Christ, my Savior and Guide, without whom this story would not have been told. I love you!

Additional thanks go to my dear friends, Rose and Leenie, who kicked my backside into gear and then helped me plan a schedule to get this book finished.

I can't ignore my wonderful cold readers, Gail and Cheryl, who keen eyes and wonderful insights and advice made the story infinitely better.

Huge thanks go to my Patreon Patrons, whose generous and unflagging support inspires me to continue.

Finally, thank you to Paul Panak, owner, designer, and chief bottle washer at Burn Knives and pastor of New Life Christian Center in Kinsman, Ohio, for generously sharing his knowledge of stilettos with me. Your sermons aren't half-bad either. ;)

Prologue

Dear Lizzy,

My visit with my godmother is going very well. I now understand better why you are so fond of coming to London. There is so much here to see and do! It is more diverting than I ever thought possible!

My aunt is a wonderful woman. She reminds me of you with her clever remarks and the way she makes sport of those around her. I think you would like her very much. I cannot imagine why we have not been to her house before, although I think it would be disrespectful of me to ask my parents to explain. It is likely none of my concern.

I have been to Gunter's twice with Aunt for ices, and four times to Hatchards. My aunt did insist that I buy something other than sermons. She says that she is determined to add to my liveliness. I worry at times that she wishes me to be like Lydia. She has assured me this is not so, but I wonder at it. I could not bear to be wild and untamed. I should prefer to be demure and accomplished, but if it will make Aunt Agnes happy, then I will comply.

On one of my visits to the bookshop, I met the most delightful young lady. Her name is Miss Georgiana Darcy, and she is but two or three years younger than I; about Lydia's age. She lives on Park Lane, across from Hyde Park, her parents are dead, and she has an older brother who is one of her guardians. She is such a beautiful girl! Lydia and Kitty would do well to have someone like her to emulate. But I digress.

Miss Darcy and I struck up an almost instant friendship. It was amazing when I think about it. Even before I knew the location of her home, I could tell by her gown that she was far above me. Yet, she was so friendly and obliging! She did not seem to mind at all that I am not as high as she.

She introduced her brother to my aunt and me, and then invited us for tea the next afternoon. Their home is beautiful! I had half-expected an ostentatious show of wealth, but it was not that way at all. It was a very elegant place. You would enjoy it, I think.

Oh, Lizzy, I hate to ask a favor like this, but would you come to stay with Aunt and me for a few weeks? I am overwhelmed with all that I am seeing and doing and feel that I need a sister with whom to discuss it all. I know that

Jane is going to Aunt Gardiner's to help with the new baby, and I do not want to interfere with that, nor do I wish for the help of Kitty or Lydia. You know that they ignore me, and their behavior is simply far too inappropriate for them to attend the events Aunt and I are invited to. You are the best suited, anyway. I have always felt a closer affinity to you, and I know that you, with your keen insight into characters and events, would be just the assistant I need. And, I would like to introduce you to Miss Darcy. If it helps you to decide, she would like to make your acquaintance, as well. Please say you will come!

Your loving sister,

Mary

Chapter 1

"Now, Mary, when we get to Hatchards, I want you to look for some poetry or history books. As I said last night, you are far too serious for a young lady of nine and ten. You require some lighter fare in your course of daily reading."

Mary nodded her head. "Yes, ma'am; I shall." She was not at all certain she wanted to read anything that was not a religious text, but her godmother was adamant that a young woman of her age should not be so somber; and, since the lady was hosting her for a few months, Mary felt obliged to obey.

Mary's godmother was also her paternal aunt and her father's only living family, other than the distant cousin who was set to inherit. Lady Agnes Baker, nee Bennet, was the Viscountess Watts. Her husband, who she affectionately called Lord Matt, was Lord Matthew Baker, Viscount Watts. The couple had two sons, the youngest of whom was a few years older than Mary, and no daughters. Lady Watts was thrilled to stand godmother to her middle niece, but she had had limited contact with her while raising her sons. The Honorable Mr. Geoffrey Baker and The Honorable Mr. Augustus Baker had been holy terrors as children, keeping their nanny, governess, and both parents well occupied trying to remain one step – or more, if possible – ahead of them. There had been no time, or energy, if the viscountess were to be honest, for lavishing the attention on a goddaughter the way she would have liked. She did keep in touch via letters with Mr. and Mrs. Bennet, and sent gifts, but she had been unable to take an active part in Mary's upbringing until now.

Now, Lady Watts was determined to undo the effects that nineteen years of neglect and careless, harsh words had had on her dearest girl. Mary had been in town for several days and this was their first outing.

They soon arrived at London's most famous bookseller. Mary gazed in awe at the shelves full of books, having never seen so many tomes all in one place before. And, it was not just one floor of books. She could clearly see more shelves of them above stairs, just beyond the top step. It was overwhelming; she did not know where to begin. She turned to her godmother, her confusion clear in her expression. Lady Watts chuckled before directing her niece to the section containing histories.

An indeterminate amount of time later, Mary was engrossed in a book describing England's War of the Roses when she adjusted her stance and bumped into someone behind her.

"Oh! I am sorry!" she exclaimed, turning around.

The young lady behind her turned, as well. "Please, forgive me. I was not paying attention."

"No, please, miss. It was I who should have watched where I was going."

The well-turned-out young woman tilted her head, smiling softly at Mary. "May I ask your name?"

Mary's eyes widened. "My name is Miss Mary Bennet." She curtseyed, for she could see that the other girl was above her in circumstance.

"I am Miss Georgiana Darcy," she replied as she returned Mary's curtsey. "I am pleased to make your acquaintance. Do you come here often?"

"No, though I wish I did. It is such a wonderful place!" Mary looked around her at the massive amount of reading material in the room. "I am here with my godmother. She is determined to expand my mind by extensive reading. She insisted I find some histories today."

Miss Darcy laughed softly, her hand over her mouth. "Yes, it is wonderful, and my brother shares your godmother's philosophy, I am afraid. I am here with my companion, searching for a book about the War of the Roses. Have you seen one, by any chance?"

The lady's chatter had calmed Mary's nervousness a bit, for she could tell that they were both anxious. "Indeed, I have. The tome I was examining when I stepped back into you is about that exact war. Here, you may have it."

"Only if there is a second copy. You found it first, and it should be yours." She rolled her eyes. "It would not trouble me in the least to report to my brother that no such books were to be found!"

Both girls giggled at this. Happily, there was a second copy of the book, and the pair, having decided they quite liked each other, sat at a small table to have a pot of tea and a chat. Their beverage had just been delivered when Lady Watts approached.

"Mary, I see you have made a friend. Might I ask you to introduce me?" She was pleased to learn that her niece's new friend was a gentle-woman of such high standing. She joined them at the table, gesturing to the footman for another cup. Though they were soon joined by Miss Darcy's companion, Mrs. Annesley, Lady Watts still managed to subtly question Mary's new acquaintance about her family and education, at the same time passing on to Miss Darcy valuable information about Mary's connections.

Noticing that the time was approaching when they must return home, Miss Darcy invited her new friend and Lady Watts for tea at her home, Darcy House, the next day.

The next afternoon, Mary and her godmother arrived at Darcy House precisely on time. They were introduced to Miss Darcy's brother. Mary found him to be rather quiet, but also very intelligent. He quizzed her about her family, but that was to be expected, as it was his duty to ensure his sister's companions were of good character. He engaged Lady Watts in a discussion about the war with France and other political matters. He spoke well and with firmness, indicating his belief that his opinions were correct. In addition, he revealed that he had a sense of humor, though it was not displayed in loud peals of mirth. As the discussion between herself, Miss Darcy, Lady Watts, and Mr. Darcy continued, Mary began to realize that the gentleman would be a perfect mate for Elizabeth. She pushed this realization to the back of her mind for the time being. She would need to examine it more closely when she was alone and had time for contemplation.

As she readied herself for bed that night, Mary thought more about Elizabeth and Mr. Darcy. *I have to get them in the same room! But how?* She knew she could not simply write her sister and demand she come to London and allow herself to be introduced to a total stranger. Lizzy was a stubborn soul, independent and strong-willed. Getting her to town would require finesse. Mary was not certain she would be able to manage on her own. She thought about asking her new friend for help, but quickly realized that Miss Darcy might think it an imposition. She might not want her brother to be connected with a family like Mary's, and such a request might damage their fledgling friendship. She determined that she would bide her time and simply observe for now. She could always invite Lizzy later and find a way for them to meet.

Over the next few weeks, Georgiana and Mary became quite close, and one could almost always be found with the other. Mary remained observant, and though she did not often have contact with her friend's brother, each time she did, her determination that he and Lizzy would suit each other very well was cemented.

Mr. Darcy himself was charmed by his sister's awkward new friend. He was relieved to hear of her connection to Viscount Watts and his wife. While he did not know them personally, they had a good reputation. No hint of scandal had attached to their name, and they were known to be moral and upright people. Miss Bennet herself was sincere, if a bit sour for his taste, but Georgiana appeared to adore her. The pair could be found together for a portion of every day, either at Darcy House or the Watts' residence, called Arthur Place, chattering like magpies about anything and everything.

Darcy had spent much time getting to know Lord and Lady Watts. The first time Georgiana was invited, he escorted her to their home, which was just one street over from his own, so that he could familiarize himself with the family. He had a duty to his sister, and after her near-elopement this past spring, he was extremely vigilant about those she came into contact with. He had barely averted scandal once; he might not be so lucky a second time. Rakes and scoundrels were found at all levels of society and he needed to sketch the characters of everyone his dear sister met. He was relieved to find the viscount, viscountess, and Miss Bennet charming and sincere. They were exactly the sort of people he would want Georgiana to spend time with; and so she did, with his blessing.

Over the course of their many conversations, Mary and Georgiana had described their families to each other, sharing annoyances and concerns alike. To the former's delight, the latter gave her an opening to introduce a much-desired conversation.

"I worry about Fitzwilliam. He is such a good brother to me, far better than I deserve, and he is so lonely. He denies it, of course, but I see the looks on his face in the evenings when he thinks I am not watching. He needs a wife."

Mary tilted her head. "Are there not ladies in his circle that would have him?"

Georgiana rolled her eyes. "Oh, there certainly are. However, the ladies of our society are not warm and welcoming, and I strongly suspect they want him only for what he can do for them."

"Do for them? What do you mean?"

"My brother's fortune is ... well, he is very well-off, and we do not want for anything. The ladies of our acquaintance look at him and see only his fortune. They do not care about *him*." She sighed. "Many of the girls I thought were my friends in school come to visit and seem to want to talk about my brother and nothing else. I have been so happy to have met you; you are interested in me and not Fitzwilliam!"

"It is difficult to not be interested in you. You are so friendly, and I confess that I greatly admire you. I had not thought to ever meet someone who had so much in common with me yet was so far above me."

"Nonsense! You are a gentleman's daughter, same as me. Fitzwilliam and I have both learned from our father to judge a man, or in this case, a young lady, by what is on the inside of him and not his social position. Papa was kind to everyone. He made friends everywhere, even with tradesmen. Our aunts and uncles look down on them; Fitzwilliam says they are stuck in the old way of thinking and that, eventually, they will have to adjust. He says times are changing, and we must keep up.

"His friend, Mr. Bingley, is from trade. He went to Cambridge with my brother, though, and inherited a large sum from his father with the intention that he purchase an estate and become landed gentry. You will like him, Mr. Bingley, I mean. He is very amiable. His sisters are ... not as friendly." Georgiana sighed again. "His younger sister would like to marry Fitzwilliam. I can see it in her eyes when they visit."

"Would you like that?"

"Oh, no! She is similar to the other ladies I told you about. She cares not for my brother, only for his fortune and the position she would gain as his wife." Suddenly, Georgiana grasped Mary's hand. "How I wish he would meet someone like you! I confess that, if I thought for a moment you were interested, I would play matchmaker."

Mary, surprised and embarrassed, squeezed her friend's hand before replying. "Well, he is very handsome and gentlemanly, but I admit that he is a little old for my taste." She paused a moment, wondering if she dared give voice to her desire to introduce Mr. Darcy to Elizabeth.

Georgiana could see that Mary had something on her mind, and encouraged her to speak.

"My older sister, Elizabeth ... the one I call Lizzy?" She looked at her companion and, seeing her nod, took a deep breath and continued. "I have thought ... I think ... every time I see your brother, I think that he and Lizzy would be a good match. I have not said anything because I do not want to be like the other ladies of your acquaintance who only befriend you to get close to your brother." Mary was worried, very much so, that Georgiana would be offended. "I value your friendship very much and would never do anything to jeopardize it, so I have kept my thoughts to myself until now."

"No, no ... it is fine. Tell me again about this particular sister. Do you really think she and Fitzwilliam would like each other?"

"I do. Lizzy is very intelligent. Sometimes too much so, I think. She always finds something to say and never lets anyone intimidate her.

She does not tolerate fools well. She is very pretty but does not let it go to her head. She is kind to everyone, even those she dislikes. She is my favorite sister, to tell the truth."

Georgiana was intrigued with the idea of becoming Mary's sister through Miss Elizabeth Bennet. Based upon her friend's description, Miss Elizabeth was someone who could easily stand up to Fitzwilliam when necessary and not be cowed by his moods. "And she is in Hertfordshire?"

"Yes, she remained at Longbourn with the rest of my family."

"Would she come if you asked her to?"

Mary shrugged. "She might; I do not know. I could not tell her that I want her to meet a gentleman. She would immediately dismiss the notion and stay at home. But, I could not lie, either."

"True." Georgiana was disappointed for a brief moment, until another idea popped into her head. "What if ... what if you told her you wanted her to meet me?"

Mary's face brightened. "I could do that! It would not be a falsehood, for I do very much want my favorite sister to meet my new friend!"

"And if that friend's brother just happened to be home when your sister met me ..."

"Exactly! Excellent idea! Will you help me write the letter? I could do it right now, and post it when I get back to Arthur Place."

"I will help you write it! Come; let us sit here by the window. The writing desk is already set up there."

The girls sat down together to compose the letter to Elizabeth. Once written, Mary put it in her reticule to post from her godmother's house. She and Georgiana eagerly discussed the future, and what they expected to happen once Elizabeth met Fitzwilliam.

As soon as Mary got back to Arthur Place, she put her letter on the salver in the entry with the rest of the outgoing post.

"Are you writing home, Mary?"

Her aunt's voice startled her. She had not expected anyone to be down at this time of day. "Yes, ma'am. I have written to Lizzy, asking her to come to town. I- I did not think you would mind."

"Of course not, my dear! It is to be expected that you might wish to see a sister or two after being away from them for so long."

"I do, but ... I admit that I have an ulterior motive."

Lady Watts' brows rose. "You do? Will you share it with me?"

Looking around to make sure no one was near to overhear, Mary edged closer to her godmother. "I believe that Lizzy and Mr. Darcy would suit each other very well. I wish for them to meet. I did not tell Lizzy this, of course, because that would be the surest way to turn her off him before they ever met, so I simply told her that I should like her to meet Miss Darcy."

Lady Watts nodded, tapping her finger on her lip. "You know, I think you might be right about that. Tell you what, grab that letter back off the pile, and come with me. I will write your father and add my desires for your sister to attend you. I will not mention Mr. Darcy to him, for you know he would take great amusement in telling your sister and that would ruin everything. I will have my husband's courier deliver the letters in the morning. How does that sound to you?"

"Oh, Aunt, that would be lovely! Thank you for your help."

Together, Mary and her godmother composed a note to Mr. Bennet. Handing the missives off to the courier with instructions to deliver them as early as possible tomorrow, they retired to dress for dinner. Mary was happy to have her letter sent on its way and anxiously awaited a reply. To her relief, a response arrived from Longbourn the very next evening.

Longbourn

"Elizabeth." Mr. Bennet called out as his second eldest daughter walked past the door to his book room. "Come here, my child, and have a seat."

Elizabeth Bennet, Lizzy to her family and Eliza to her closest friend, entered the room, seating herself in her favorite chair beside her father's desk.

"Good afternoon, Papa," she greeted with a smile. "Is something wrong? You do not often invite us into your sanctuary at this time of day."

Mr. Bennet chuckled. This room was, indeed, his place of refuge from an excitable wife and five daughters, and it was rare that any were invited in. Except for Lizzy, of course; she was his favorite and was welcomed more often than the rest.

Elizabeth was twenty years old. She lived with her family, consisting of her parents and four sisters, on the family's estate, which was called Longbourn. The eldest of the girls, Jane, was two and twenty. Next came Elizabeth, and following her was Mary, who was nineteen, Kitty, who was seventeen, and Lydia, who was fifteen.

Longbourn had been in the Bennet family for hundreds of years. It was small but well maintained, with an income of about two thousand pounds per annum. This revenue was enough to meet expenses and allow the family to live a very good life, as befit their status. The girls had access to whatever masters they desired to further their education, Mr. Bennet had all the port and books he wished for, and Mrs. Bennet was able to clothe her daughters well and entertain to her heart's content. There was, however, nothing left over to add to either savings or dowries for Elizabeth and her sisters. The young ladies would all receive equal shares of

Mrs. Bennet's dowry, and that only after their parents had passed.

All the Bennets enjoyed living on the estate, for theirs was an elegant home filled with love and laughter, and the fussing and fighting that came along with six women all residing together. It was, however, entailed upon the male line and none of the ladies would inherit. The heir presumptive, a distant cousin to Mr. Bennet named William Collins, was unknown to them. Mr. Bennet had been connected to the man's father when he was a child, before the two branches of the family had a falling out and severed acquaintance with each other. Without knowledge of the kind of person this heir was, there was no guarantee that he would allow Mrs. Bennet and her daughters to remain on the estate after Mr. Bennet's passing.

Such uncertainty was the mistress' undoing. Mrs. Bennet was left, after birthing five daughters and no sons, with what she delicately called "a nervous condition" that left her with flutterings and spasms all over her person when situations became too much for her. Usually, this meant that she had not gotten her way in some manner or another.

Mr. Bennet himself generally took to his book room when his wife had a spell. He had perfected the art of announcing whatever news he was duty bound to share with them and then vanishing immediately, leaving his daughters to deal with their mother.

Thomas Bennet did not limit his avoidance to his wife's fits of nerves, however. Sitting in his book room reading his newest tome was his preferred occupation. He was not fond of society in general, though he did gain much amusement from observing his neighbors at the various dinners, assemblies, and private balls held in the area. Nor was he particularly keen on being out amongst his tenants. He had a steward to do the actual work of running the estate, and beyond providing funds and resolving the occasional dispute amongst his renters, he had little to do with it. Likewise, he left the raising of his five children to his wife. He preferred his own company to that of anyone or anything else. If he must exert himself, he would prefer to do it spending time with Elizabeth.

While all of his daughters had access to his library, only Elizabeth made full use of his books. Jane had restricted herself to poetry and the occasional novel, Mary to sermons, and the youngest two preferred any activity to reading. His second eldest, however, had read every book he owned. She was a quick study, easily grasping the most complicated matters. She had also inherited his quick wit and tendency to sarcasm. The two had spent many a cold winter's evening in debate over some topic or other, and more and more often did Elizabeth prove her opinion to be the soundest.

His wife, of course, did not appreciate his encouragement of her least understood daughter in the matter of improving her mind. Elizabeth, with her preference for books and solitary walks about the countryside, baffled Mrs. Bennet, and she was certain no gentleman would ever have her for a wife. All of her husband's explanations that some men preferred an intelligent spouse went over her head. She had not caught a husband with her mind, but with her beauty and lively personality, and she could not fathom anything else. Furthermore, she did not know who would maintain the girl when her father was gone, for Mrs. Bennet herself would not have the funds.

Elizabeth had learned to ignore her mother's frequent lectures, for the most part. It bothered her, of course, to be berated so often for something so innocuous, but she could not bring herself to be disrespectful by talking back. She did love her Mama, despite Mrs. Bennet's inability to control her speech or regulate her voice in public, traits which often embarrassed her daughters.

To be honest, as much as Elizabeth appreciated her father's interest in her and his willingness to help her education along, and as much as she loved him in return, she found herself frequently wishing he would act to control his family. Her youngest sister was wild and untamed, and Kitty followed wherever Lydia led with no thought to her own reputation. Mary, in an effort to distinguish herself, poured her efforts into the pianoforte and making extracts of sermons. She gave the impression that she was a self-righteous prig when, in fact, she was simply an uncertain young lady trying to appear intelligent. Her father, should he take the time and effort to do so, could, with just a few words, improve Mary's outlook enough to possibly change her behavior, yet he failed to do so. It would take a more concerted effort to alter the manners of Kitty and Lydia, but with diligence, it could be accomplished. She knew, however, that Mr. Bennet would not be moved from his book room and since she was not formed for un-happiness, Elizabeth did what she could to influence those around her, pasted a smile on her face, and walked out whenever she found opportunity. It was from one of these daily strolls that she was returning when she was beckoned to join her father.

"No, nothing is the matter. Not yet, at any rate, but your mother has not come down from her rooms." Mr. Bennet chuckled at his own jest, while Elizabeth smiled and shook her head.

"Papa."

Returning Elizabeth's smile, Mr. Bennet began his explanation for summoning her. "Have you received your post today?"

"No, I have not, not as of yet." It was unusual for her father to inquire after her correspond-ence, and she was surprised that he did so now.

"I suspect you will have a letter from your younger sister, asking that you attend her in town."

Elizabeth's brows rose. "Really? Does she say why?" She was not terribly surprised by the request. Mary had always preferred her to either their older or younger sisters. What did surprise her was that Mary wanted anyone at all with her. She had been quite eager to be away from them, and now Elizabeth worried that something had happened to upset her in some manner.

"She does not, but your aunt has sent me a note to warn me of the request. She reassures me that nothing is wrong and that your sister appears to be enjoying herself. She has made a new friend, and I think perhaps she wishes to get your opinion on the matter. Are you interested in going?" He peered at her over his spectacles. He knew how protective his girls were of each other, and was quite certain that his Lizzy would not hesitate to go to Mary.

"I am. It is an unexpected request, to be sure, but my sister would not ask if she did not truly need me."

"Very well, then. I shall send an express to your aunt. You may take my carriage to the post stop tomorrow. She will send hers to meet you there. Your mother and sisters can chaperone you as far as the posting inn; I am quite certain they would enjoy a bit of shopping as recompense for staying at Longbourn."

"Thank you, Papa. I will begin my packing now." Elizabeth rose from her chair, walking around behind his desk to kiss his cheek before heading toward the door.

"I shall miss you, Daughter. You are the most sensible of my children, you know. What shall I do while you are gone?"

Elizabeth turned before exiting the room, an impish grin on her face. "Why, I do not know what you will do!" she exclaimed, before winking and stepping into the hall to the sound of her father's delighted laughter.

Chapter 2

London

"Mary, dear," Lady Watts called out as she entered the drawing room. "I have a letter from your father."

"You do? What does he say?"

Lady Watts laughed. "That was a rapid response! I have never seen you so eager to hear from your family."

Mary blushed at her godmother's tease. "Yes, well, I have never before had as good a reason for it."

Laughing once more, the lady relayed the news. "Your sister will arrive tomorrow in time for tea. Would you like to invite Miss Darcy, or do you think Elizabeth will want to rest today and meet your friend later?"

"Oh, I cannot imagine Lizzy being too tired to meet someone new, but I confess I should like some time to visit with her before we have guests." Mary looked at her hands, clasped in her lap. "I have never been from home for so long, and though I have been without my elder sisters for longer periods, this time feels different. I am impatient to be with her."

Lady Watts laid her hand over her goddaughter's. Speaking gently, she reassured her. "Of course you are. This is all so new to you, being in London and in society. It is good that Elizabeth is coming to give you a listening ear and help you sort things out in your mind." She leaned over and kissed Mary's cheek. "You are a beautiful young woman, and I am so happy to be able to host you." Squeezing the hand she held, Lady Watts smiled before rising, quietly leaving her guest to contemplate her sister's coming.

The time between Mr. Bennet's express and Elizabeth's arrival passed as it always does when someone is expecting an eagerly-awaited visitor. That is to say, rather slowly. Eventually, though, Lizzy entered the house to be eagerly embraced by her aunt, uncle, and sister, who clung to her as though she might never let go.

"Oh Lizzy, I am so happy to see you!"

"And I, you. Are you well? Your letter worried me."

"I am sorry; I did not mean to cause you alarm. It is just that I missed you and am in need of a sisterly ear to listen and help me make sense of my thoughts and feelings."

Elizabeth searched Mary's face for the truth. Not seeing any artifice, she conceded. "Very well, then. We shall talk this evening before bed, as we do at Longbourn, yes?"

"Oh, yes, thank you, Lizzy!" With a final hug, the girls broke apart and followed Lord and Lady Watts to the drawing room, where tea was laid out. Following a lively discussion and catching up of news, the group separated to prepare for dinner.

It was much later that evening that the house retired. Mary soon knocked on Elizabeth's door, and upon being invited in, settled on the bed as she was wont to do at home when the sisters chatted.

"I am so happy you have come, Lizzy!"

"I am, as well." Elizabeth leaned forward to place her hand on Mary's. "Is anything bothering you? You do not seem out of sorts, but I was surprised that you requested me to come."

"Truly," Mary began in an earnest tone of voice, "I am happy. My aunt is wonderful to me, and treats me as her own child. I have been to dinners and the theater and museums, and had so many new experiences! I simply needed a sister with whom to share them."

Elizabeth laughed. "Well, then, here I am. Tell me all about it."

They spent a happy hour with the younger sister describing in great detail her adventures.

The next day

"Lizzy, with my godmother's permission, I have invited my friend, Georgiana, to dine this evening."

"Wonderful! I am pleased. You have needed a friend, and I am happy you have found one. You make her sound lovely."

"Oh, she is!"

"Indeed, she is," interjected Lady Watts. "Shy and lovely, and of the best of families."

"Good, good. What can you tell me about her?"

Mary explained all that she knew about Georgiana, including that she had a brother. Purposely, Mary did not tell her sister that said brother was unmarried or that she and her friend hoped to push them together. She wanted their meeting to be totally without prejudice.

~~~***~~~

Elizabeth and Mary descended the staircase together, dressed in their finest and chatting about the evening's guests and entertainment. After spending the morning practicing on the pianoforte, they were prepared to perform a duet, along with individual performances.

"I do hope we can convince our aunt to display, as well. She is quite skilled, you know."

"Then I will do my best to persuade her. What about Miss Darcy? You said that she is a gifted performer, as well."

"She is, but she is not yet out and is quite shy. I am not certain she will be willing, though we can certainly ask."

Elizabeth smiled. "Very well, we will not push her."

At that moment, they arrived at the drawing room, where their aunt and uncle awaited them. Before they had a chance to settle into
~~~

seats, the butler, Mr. Clarke, stepped into the room and announced the visitors.

"Mr. Fitzwilliam Darcy and Miss Georgiana Darcy."

"Mr. Darcy, Miss Darcy, welcome! Come in, come in." Lord Watts greatly enjoyed being a host and was eager to get the evening underway.

"Thank you for inviting us, sir." Mr. Darcy began, his attention focused on the viscount. "My sister and I have been eagerly awaiting this event."

"Wonderful!" Lord Watts turned to his family. "The ladies have done nothing but chatter about it all day, as well."

Darcy smiled as he, too, turned his attention to the ladies. He greeted his hostess and his sister's friend, then noticed a new person standing beside Miss Bennet. He was struck by her sparkling, laughing eyes and the half-smile that graced her face. Not removing his gaze from her, he asked his host for an introduction.

"Certainly! This is another of my nieces, Mary's older sister, Miss Elizabeth Bennet. Elizabeth, this is Mr. Fitzwilliam Darcy."

Darcy reached out to grasp Elizabeth's hand. Bowing over it, he resisted the urge to kiss it, instead forcing himself to stand up but retaining the delicate appendage in his grasp. "I am pleased to meet you, Miss Bennet."

Elizabeth startled at the sound of his deep voice. She blushed, curtseying and returning his greeting. Her attention had been riveted by the tall, handsome man when he entered the room, and his warm touch made her heart race. For that reason, she made no move to pull her hand away, though she knew very well that she should.

Mary and Georgiana exchanged glances, relaying to each other their happiness with the events of the evening so far. Of course, this was just a first meeting; there was still work to do to be assured an attachment would form, but so far, it seemed as though the couple in question was going to make it very easily done.

Lord and Lady Watts also exchanged amused glances. In the way that long-married couples often had, they communicated their delight at the apparent fascination Elizabeth had with Mr. Darcy, and he with her. They silently agreed to discuss it later, but both knew that it was an eligible match.

The spell that held Darcy and Elizabeth in thrall was broken by Mr. Clarke, who once again entered the room, this time to announce that dinner was served. The couple jumped apart, blushing deeply, and Darcy quickly introduced his sister to the newcomer. That nicety completed, the group paired up, with Lord Watts quickly taking his wife's arm and Darcy, while surprised that the elder couple had chosen not to follow propriety's rules for precedence, gladly offering his to Elizabeth. Mary and Georgiana followed at the rear, trying to contain their giggles.

Darcy received a further surprise when, instead of entering the formal dining room, Lord Watts led them into a parlor that had been set up as an intimate dining space. The small table just fit the six of them without feeling cramped. Darcy was seated at the right hand of his host, with Elizabeth to his right. Georgiana was seated to the right of Lady Watts, and Mary was across from Darcy.

The evening progressed as most dinner parties do, but the further along it went, the harder pressed Darcy was to give his attention to anyone but the woman beside him. He was intrigued by her conversation and witty banter.

Elizabeth was just as interested in Darcy. While she found him to be very formal in all their interactions, he displayed an interest in what she had to say and a respect for her opinions that she had never before experienced. It became, over the course of their conversation, a challenge for her to make the hint of his smile appear, and she took it as a personal accomplishment when she managed it.

Too soon for either of them, the evening ended. As they said good night, Darcy spoke quietly to Elizabeth. "May I call on you, Miss Bennet?"

Elizabeth was surprised and pleased. "You may."

"Thank you." His appreciation was clear in his voice and manner as he bowed over her hand once again.

As she got ready for bed that evening, after enduring the sly innuendoes of her family and their probing questions about her opinion of Mr. Darcy, Elizabeth let herself examine the evening and her dinner companion.

She was impressed with the gentleman, she had to admit. He was attentive to her, but other men had been in the past. What intrigued her more was that he did not scoff at her opinions. He challenged her to explain them more fully at times, and debated them at others, but never did he belittle them.

He was gentle with her to the point of tenderness. She searched her mind for anyone of her acquaintance, including her family, who treated her so, and could not think of a single person, male or female, who did. She found that she rather enjoyed being the recipient of such attentions, and was glad he was to call on her.

Elizabeth had long ago realized her limited prospects at home. Everyone there knew of her small portion. They were well acquainted with her likes and dislikes, her pursuits and passions, and her sharp wit. Even if there were gentlemen of the right age and consequence, not too old or too young – which there were not – she was not able to compete with other women who had more beauty or a bigger dowry. She had nothing but her wit and her charm with which to entice a gentleman. Finally, there were few newcomers to the area. She had begun to fear that she would never marry, or would have to marry a tradesman and give up the luxuries she enjoyed as a gentleman's daughter. Worse, she feared a marriage without esteem, respect, or affection. Given these facts, if Mr. Darcy continued to call, it would be a blessing that she would not take for granted.

The same night, Darcy House ...

Darcy dismissed his valet, Mr. Smith, and climbed into his large, empty bed. His thoughts were full of Miss Elizabeth Bennet, as they had been since he first laid eyes on her at Arthur Place.

Never had he been so captivated by a woman. He had been master of his family's estate for five years, taking the reins at the death of his father. At every turn after that – even before then, if he were honest – he had been pursued by many women. He had danced with hundreds of them, but none had held his attention for longer than a set. Miss Bennet, however, had. He mentally listed her good qualities: she was vivacious, good humored, intelligent, accomplished on the pianoforte, had expanded her mind by extensive reading, spoke and read French, and read Latin and Greek. She played chess, and was able to hold her own in a debate. Her opinions were well thought out. Beyond her mind, her person was attractive, as well. Her figure was light and pleasing, and her eyes were expressive.

There was none of the bored debutante about her, with cold eyes and blank looks. She exuded warmth, and it drew him to her like a bee to a flower.

Darcy turned his mind to her connections and circumstances. Her aunt and uncle were peers, and that was in her favor. It was unfortunate that her mother's family was from trade, but he had learned long ago not to judge a person based on his position in society.

It was also unfortunate that she had so little by way of a dowry. While he did not know the exact figure, Lord Watts had told him that the Bennet sisters would have equal shares in their mother's portion after her death, and that was all. Their father had not saved to add to that amount. Of course, Darcy was wealthy enough that it did not matter much to him; his concern was his family's reaction. While he did not cater to their whims, wants, or desires, and would marry whomever he chose without regard for their opinion, he did not want his future wife to be treated poorly because she was not from the same circles. *I shall have to make it plain to them, should I choose Miss Bennet, that she is to be treated with the same accord they would have treated my mother, had she lived. And I am almost certain I shall eventually offer for her; she is everything I have looked for in a wife.* With those pleasant thoughts, Darcy drifted off to sleep, a smile on his face.

The very next day found Darcy and his sister knocking on the door of Arthur Place. They were immediately granted entrance, Clarke taking their hats and gloves and handing them off to a maid before escorting the Darcys to the drawing room. Georgiana and Mary, after observing the niceties and greeting everyone, sped off to the pianoforte to practice and observe. Lady Watts rang for tea, and she, her niece, and Darcy arranged themselves on the sofas, with Darcy claiming the seat next to Elizabeth, Lady Watts sitting across from them.

"My husband sends his apologies, Mr. Darcy. He wanted to be here to visit with you, but was called away on an unexpected matter at Parliament."

"Please relay to him my understanding. At times, I, too, have been summoned unexpectedly and forced to miss visitors I greatly desired to see."

The tea arrived just then, and Lady Watts set about pouring out for everyone. The younger girls, called away from the instrument to partake, accepted their cups but hurried back to their previous location, so as not to miss a moment of whispered conversation and giggles.

The group on the sofas spent the next hour, far beyond what was the usually acceptable time, chatting. They discussed books this day, Darcy and Elizabeth discovering that they had similar but not identical tastes. Lady Watts took part in the conversation when called upon, but for the most part, she simply sat back and let the young people talk.

While Darcy and the older ladies were thus engaged, Georgiana and Mary were practicing on the room's pianoforte and conducting their own discussion. They whispered to each other observations on how well Darcy and Elizabeth looked together and how they got on so well, and giggled often about their lack of attention to anyone and anything else but each other. The girls were greatly encouraged that the match would be made, and with little effort on their parts.

Before taking his leave, Darcy invited Elizabeth to accompany him on an outing on the morrow.

"Have you ever visited Kensington Gardens, Miss Bennet?"

"I have not, though I have always wished to. My uncle Gardiner has never had the time to spare when I have visited, and as I have already shared with you, my father does not much like to visit town, so he has not brought us either."

"If it would please you, I should like to invite you and your sister along with Georgiana and me tomorrow. Of course, Lord and Lady Watts are included in the invitation, should they wish to come."

"Oh, I should greatly enjoy it!" Turning to her aunt, Elizabeth added, "I must defer to Lady Watts, of course."

"Of course we will go! Well, I shall, at any rate. Lord Watts will if he is able. My husband and I greatly enjoy the gardens and had hoped to visit while Elizabeth was here. Thank you for your kind invitation."

Darcy bowed. "It is nothing, I assure you. Shall we all ride in my carriage? Georgiana and I can be here at, say, noon, to pick up your party?"

"Excellent! We shall be ready and waiting!"

Elizabeth's aunt gave her a nudge, causing her to realize she had been staring at Darcy. "I look forward to it." She gave him her hand and watched as he bent over it, wishing as he did that he would kiss the fingers so she could discover the softness of his lips.

Little did she know that Darcy wished for the same thing and that it was only with the greatest of effort that he was able to control his impulses and behave in a gentlemanlike manner. He tore himself away with his heart pounding, bowing again and wishing the ladies a good afternoon, before shepherding his sister out the door.

When their guests were gone and they had resumed their seats, Lady Watts and Mary turned to Elizabeth with matching smiles.

"So, Lizzy ... what do you think of my friend's brother? He is very handsome, would you not agree?"

Elizabeth blushed to the roots of her hair. She cleared her throat. "Indeed, he is. He is a very nice gentleman, and I am glad to have the opportunity to get to know him."

"He would be a very good match for you, you know," her aunt pointed out. "Mr. Darcy is well respected and has a handsome fortune. I doubt you could do better were you to set your cap at a peer."

"As you know, I am largely indifferent to fortune. I wish to marry someone I respect and esteem. I do not need a great deal of money; I have not grown up with abundant riches. And, while I would rather not go lower and do without the servants and things I am accustomed to, I do not require more." She paused, not wanting to give away too much because she was not certain of her feelings. "I like him very much. I am eager to learn more of him, and ... well ... I should just like to know him better. That is all I will say at present."

Lady Watts nodded. "Very well, we shall not tease you further. I encourage you, though, to take this time to judge his behavior, and his pursuits and passions, and see if they match your desires. It truly is an eligible match for you, and I would hate to see you pass it up." She stood, and the girls rose with her. "I believe I shall rest in my rooms for a while. I give you both leave to pursue whatever activities you would like, though I do ask that, if you leave the house, you take a footman along with you for protection. One cannot be too careful here in town, even in a neighborhood like Mayfair."

"Yes, Aunt."

"We shall."

They curtsied and watched their aunt retreat from the room. By mutual agreement, they spent the remaining hours of the afternoon in the library, alternately reading and chatting about all the things they would like to do while staying in the house of Mary's godmother.

The following day's visit to Kensington Gardens was delightful for the entire party. Lord Watts was able to join them, and conversation flowed freely amongst them.

From that day forward, it was not only Georgiana Darcy that could be found in the vicinity of Mary Bennet. Since Mary and Elizabeth were always together, and Darcy visited Elizabeth daily, it was Darcy as well as his sister who could always be found in the company of the Bennets and their relations. For several weeks, his daily calls continued. Often, he would invite Elizabeth and her family for outings, to the museum or for a walk in Hyde Park, and once to a ball.

Those outings always involved talks with Elizabeth, who Darcy found to be more fascinating the longer he knew her. Finally, the day came when he knew he wanted to ask her to marry him. He was reasonably certain she would accept based on her looks when he entered the room she was in, her expressions when she gazed at him without knowing he saw her, and her responses to his touch, which had gotten a bit bolder over the weeks.

Darcy wanted to create a special atmosphere in which to make his proposal. He decided to host her and her family for dinner, and enlisted his sister to help him plan it.

Chapter 3

"Georgiana." Darcy walked into the breakfast room. "I need you to do me a favor."

Georgiana looked up from the sideboard, where she was filling a plate, her eyes wide. It was a rare thing for her brother to request anything of her. "Certainly; you only need ask."

Picking up his own plate, Darcy joined her. "I want to hold a dinner party. Will you organize it for me?"

Alarm spread over Georgiana, and her eyes grew wide. "I have never done anything of that nature before. I, I, I-"

"Did school not teach you such things?"

"Well, yes, we had lessons on entertaining but that is hardly the same thing as actually arranging one!"

"Then this shall be practice for you, will it not?" Seeing her doubtful look, Darcy continued. "I have every confidence in you. Mrs. Annesley is here to help you. It will be just a small party in attendance: the Miss Bennets, Lord and Lady Watts, us, and Bingley. Oh! And the Gardiners and Jane Bennet, as well." Darcy and Georgiana had met Mary and Elizabeth's aunt and uncle Gardiner the day before, and were aware that the eldest Bennet daughter was due to arrive in London in another day or two.

"Not Mr. Bingley's family? Just him?"

Darcy cleared his throat. His sister was unaware of Miss Bingley's recent attempt to force him to marry her, and he had no intention of informing her. "Yes, just Bingley. Miss Bingley is attending a house party with friends, and Mr. and Mrs. Hurst are visiting his father's estate."

Georgiana nodded. "Very well, then. To be honest, I am happy to hear it. They make me uncomfortable, and I do not like the way Miss Bingley behaves as though she owns this house when she is here."

"No, I do not like it either, but I did not realize you were uncomfortable with them. Why did you not tell me?"

"Mr. Bingley is your friend. It pleased you to have him here and that meant having his sisters, as well." She shrugged. "I could bear it for your sake."

"Well, thank you. I hope, though, that you no longer will need to. I do not see Bingley's sisters visiting anymore. Not Miss Bingley, at any rate."

Georgiana's brows rose at this, but she knew better than to question her brother. If she needed to know, he would tell her. He would not appreciate impertinence on her part, and inquiring into his business would most certainly been seen as such. "Well, then. I will plan for nine. Should I invite someone else, or will Mrs. Annesley do to give us an even number at table?"

Darcy paused, thinking. "Mrs. Annesley is a good choice. You will then have her guidance as you serve as hostess for the evening."

The pair had moved to the table while they were talking, and began to eat as Darcy laid out his desires for the event. Setting a date for three days hence, they decided that Georgiana would write out the invitations and plan the menu after breaking her fast, and take them to her brother, who would give final approval to the menu and send a messenger to deliver the notes.

The longer they spoke and the clearer her plans became, the more excited Georgiana was. It would truly be a momentous occasion for her, but given her brother's close attention to every detail, she suspected it might be for him, as well. She would discuss it with Mary when she arrived today to visit. *Brother will keep Miss Bennet occupied, I am sure. Perhaps I will ask Mary to help me with the planning.*

~~~***~~~

While Darcy and his sister were discussing their dinner party, Elizabeth and Mary received word that their eldest sister, Jane, had arrived at the Gardiners' house on Gracechurch Street. They sent a message back to her via Lord Watts' private courier that they would call the next day.

As soon as was acceptable the following morning, Mary, Elizabeth, and Lady Watts
~~~

were knocking on the door of the Gardiner residence. Jane met them in the entrance hall rather than waiting in the drawing room.

"Lizzy!" Jane rushed to her sister, enveloping her in a hug. After a moment, they drew slightly apart, each reaching out to Mary to draw her in.

"Oh, Jane, I have missed you!"

"I have missed you, as well, dear Mary. Let me look at you." The girls separated so Jane could take in the gorgeous dress Mary was wearing. "What a beautiful gown! So elegant!"

Mary blushed at the compliment. "Thank you. Aunt Agnes insisted on purchasing me some new things. I worry that the color is too bright." Mary glanced at Lady Watts. "But she insisted that I was too young to dress somberly."

"The color is perfect! It brings out the blush in your cheeks. You are a lovely young woman, regardless of what you wear, but this gown displays it better."

"Thank you. Lizzy said much the same about the blue one I wore yesterday."

"And you know I was correct," Elizabeth teased. "By the end of your visit with our aunt, you will be so accustomed to wearing bright colors that you will never again wear drab ones."

Mary laughed. "Mama will be happy, I am sure."

Jane and Elizabeth laughed with her. Finally, Jane looked to her aunts and noted Mrs. Gardiner's pointed look toward the parlor.

"Come. Let us sit down and catch up on all your new experiences."

The ladies retired to the drawing-room, arranging themselves on the sofas and chairs in an intimate configuration while Mrs. Gardiner rang for tea. At first, they all conversed together, sharing news and jokes and laughter. Soon, though, the ladies formed smaller groups, with Lady Watts and Mrs. Gardiner conducting one conversation while Jane, Elizabeth, and Mary had another.

Mary, who had been bursting to tell the news, was the first to indicate to Jane that their sister had a suitor. "Do you recall my friend, Miss Darcy?" she asked.

"I do," her eldest sister replied. With her focus on Mary, Jane missed the blush that quickly overtook Elizabeth's features.

"She has a brother, and he has been calling on Lizzy!"

Jane laughed at the manner in which her most restrained sister displayed her excitement, which was far more like their youngest sister than her usual self. "Really?" She turned to Elizabeth. "Is this true? It must be, if I am any judge of your expressions."

"It is true. Mr. Darcy is the best of men. He is intelligent and respectful, and I greatly enjoy spending time with him."

"Have you ... reached an understanding?"

Elizabeth looked at her hands, clasped in her lap. "No," she replied softly, "but I have great hopes." She brought her eyes back up to meet her sister's just as a smile brightened Jane's countenance. "He is far above us in consequence, as Mary has noted in her letters, and he has a fair amount of pride in his estate and family, but he is friends with a tradesmen's son and kind to everyone he meets, from what I have witnessed."

"Do you love him?"

Elizabeth hesitated, but answered Jane's question. "I am uncomfortable sharing feelings with you that I may or may not have, and that I have not shared with him, but I will tell you that I greatly esteem him and respect him, and I know from his behavior that he respects and esteems me."

"If he proposed …?"

"*If* Mr. Darcy proposes, and it is not a certainty that he will, but *if* he does, I will accept him."

Jane nodded. "You are correct. Certainly, marriages have started with far less."

Thinking of their own parents, who had little in common with each other, Mary interjected her thoughts on the subject. "You are both intelligent and well-read, and enjoy a good debate. You are highly compatible; it is an eligible match for you in all aspects."

Elizabeth smiled. "It is, indeed. However, he may never ask me, and so this is all simple conjecture." She wondered at the sly smile that appeared on Mary's face at her statement, but did not have time to inquire further, as her young cousins entered the room at that point to spend time with them. By the end of the visit, it had been forgotten entirely.

~~~***~~~

On the day of the dinner, Mary could barely contain her excitement. She and Georgiana had planned this evening's entertainment very carefully, as per Darcy's directions, and had speculated eagerly on his intentions in holding it. None of the Darcy family relations had been invited and only one of his friends. Georgiana had ventured the opinion that he did not want his aunts and uncles to know, for various reasons. Having already learned that they tended to look down on those they deemed social inferiors, Mary was glad they were excluded. The girls had finally, after much discussion and conjecture, decided that Darcy was going to propose to Elizabeth. Nothing would give either of them more pleasure, and both were certain Elizabeth would accept him.

And now, on the day of the big event, footmen flew back and forth between Darcy House and Arthur Place bearing notes for Mary and Georgiana. If they could not be together all day to express their sentiments in person, they could very well do so in writing.

Lord and Lady Watts and Elizabeth observed Mary's excitement with amusement. For Elizabeth, it felt again as though someone had kidnapped her normally staid sister and replaced her with their youngest sibling. She
~~~

would never say that to Mary, though, for she enjoyed this new aspect to the other girl's personality. *Would that she had met Miss Darcy years ago,* she thought.

Finally came evening, and the residents of Arthur Place gathered in the vestibule, ready to go out. Once the Gardiner carriage arrived, they boarded their own equipage for the short trip around the corner to the Darcy residence. Upon reaching their destination, Lord Watts handed out his wife and her goddaughter before stepping back, for Darcy had presented himself at the carriage to hand out Elizabeth. With the vehicles emptied and greetings performed, the group made their way inside.

Upon entering the drawing room, where Georgiana waited with her companion and Mr. Bingley, more introductions were made. Bingley, once he laid eyes on Jane Bennet, was struck speechless. Jane was similarly affected, and her sisters could plainly see that she liked him very much. The group fell into easy conversations while they waited for dinner to be served.

Once the bell was rung, Darcy let everyone know that formal protocol was not to be followed, thus allowing him the privilege of escorting Elizabeth in to dinner. Seating her at his right hand, and with Georgiana, as hostess, at the other end of the table, he waited for everyone to find a place before he and the gentlemen sat.

Conversation flowed easily and smoothly as the courses were served. At one point, Bingley indicated he was looking for an estate to lease, and Jane remembered that the estate next to Longbourn was currently empty.

"Why, there is a house next to ours that is available for lease. The family that had been living there returned to the north several months ago. Perhaps you might look into it? It is called Netherfield. My Uncle Phillips is the solicitor in charge of it."

Bingley immediately expressed interest, vowing to put his own solicitor on the case as soon as possible the next day.

After the meal, the sexes separated for a while, as was customary. The division did not last long; Darcy was eager to be in Elizabeth's presence and get her alone, and the gentlemen all knew, or thought they knew, what his purpose was in inviting them here.

It was no surprise to the ladies, of course, when the gentlemen entered the drawing room. Mary and Georgiana began a duet to entertain the guests. While the rest of the guests were thus engaged, Darcy drew Elizabeth away from the others, where he encouraged her to sit on a sofa beside him.

"Miss Elizabeth," he began, happy that her elder sister had joined them so he could address her thusly. "I know that we have not known each other for a very long time ... it has only been a few weeks ... but ..." He looked up from their hands, which he had joined upon beginning his address. Seeing the encouragement in her eyes, he continued. "From the first moment of our acquaintance, I was struck by you, by your liveliness and intelligence. Every meeting since has cemented in my mind how very ... right you are, for me, and how well we go on together. My feelings for you have grown from fascination to something much stronger. Miss Elizabeth ... I love you. Will you marry me?"

"Oh, Mr. Darcy!" One of Elizabeth's hands had risen to cover her mouth as tears filled her eyes. "I feel the same; yes, I will happily marry you! Thank you!"

Darcy let out the breath he had not realized he was holding as his smile grew at her words. He lifted the hand he still held to his lips and graced it with a kiss. "Thank you. I will endeavor to make you very happy."

They remained at the back of the room for the rest of their sisters' performance, staring into each other's eyes and holding hands. Every once in a while, Darcy kissed her fingers. It was only when the music stopped and the room suddenly became silent that the pair realized they had become the object of attention.

"Darcy, what are the two of you doing back there!" Lord Watts' voice was jovial. It was rare that anyone had opportunity to tease Fitzwilliam Darcy and he was determined to make the most of it.

Bingley, who knew Darcy better than anyone in the room, save Georgiana, added his voice. "Yes, Darcy ... what are you being so clandestine about back there?"

Darcy and Elizabeth had startled apart at the voices calling out to them, blushing to the roots of their hair. Quickly they stood and faced their friends and family. Darcy took a deep breath, grasped Elizabeth's hand, tucked it under his elbow, and then addressed the room.

"I am beyond happy to announce that Miss Elizabeth has done me the great honor of accepting my hand in marriage."

Georgiana and Mary squealed with delight, first hugging each other, then rushing to Elizabeth. Jane was torn between laughing at one sister and congratulating the other. She settled for hugging her Aunt Gardiner.

The next day

Darcy rode to Hertfordshire early the following morning, arriving at Longbourn at midday, to an almost empty house. Bingley rode along to keep him company, hoping to get a glimpse of Netherfield. Their first stop upon arriving in Meryton was the office of Mr. Phillips, the Bennet ladies' uncle and the town's solicitor, to speak to him about Netherfield. Having been granted an appointment with the attorney to view the property later in the day, the pair rode on to the Bennet family estate.

The gentlemen were admitted to the house by a servant of middle years who Darcy assumed to be the housekeeper, and were immediately ushered into the room occupied by the master of the house.

"Mr. Fitzwilliam Darcy and Mr. Charles Bingley."

A grey-haired gentleman rose from behind the desk at one end of the book-filled room. He bowed to his visitors, who returned his greeting, before extending his hand to them. "I am pleased to make your acquaintance. I am Thomas Bennet. Welcome to Longbourn." Shaking his hand, the friends thanked him for seeing them.

"Please, have a seat." Mr. Bennet waved toward the chairs in front of the fire, coming around the desk to take one for himself. "My second daughter has mentioned you in her letters to me, Mr. Darcy. She seems quite taken with you, from what I gather."

Darcy smiled a bit. "Before I reply, let me introduce you to my friend, Charles Bingley. Your daughters just met him, at a dinner in my home, last evening. He is hoping to view Netherfield today, as he is looking to lease an estate for a while."

"Well, that is excellent news! The house has sat empty for far too long; Lord Hampton was the last person to lease it, and that was a year or more ago. My wife will be especially happy to hear of your taking it."

"Thank you, sir. I am hoping it is what I am looking for and that I may join you all here for a few months."

"Good, good!" Turning back to Darcy, Bennet continued. "Surely Netherfield is not the only reason you have decided to come visit?"

"No, sir, it is not. I am here to tell you that I have asked Miss Elizabeth to marry me and she has consented. All that remains is for me to obtain your permission." Darcy felt more nervous with each word, causing him to end in a rush. "My position in life is secure; I am the master of my estate, which is on firm financial footing, and I have a handsome fortune. I will be generous with her settlement; she will want for nothing, not in my lifetime or should I predecease her."

"Thank you for your transparency." He glanced at Bingley. "Would you like to discuss money matters now, or would you prefer a private interview for that purpose?"

"Now is fine, I think. Bingley is privy to many of my affairs, and can be trusted to keep what is said to himself."

"Very well, then. I do not know if you are aware, but Elizabeth and her sisters are to share in my wife's portion. Each will receive one thousand pounds upon her death. I have not added to it, and now that I am faced with a suitor for one of them, I must say I am a bit embarrassed about it. Will that sway you from your desire to marry my Lizzy?"

"No, sir, it will not. I have been made aware of her small portion. But, in comparison to what she does possess ... intelligence, good humor, a sharp wit, beauty ... money matters little. I can well afford a wife who comes to me as she does."

"I am happy to hear it. I would have hated to have my daughter's heart broken because of it. Before I give you my final decision, let me ask you one more thing. Do you love her?"

"I do," Darcy assured Mr. Bennet in his deep voice. "She takes my breath away."

"Excellent! Then, I give my consent. Welcome to the family."

The gentlemen shook hands, Darcy thanking his soon-to-be father-in-law, and settled into hammering out the basics of the settlement. Darcy promised to return as soon as possible with drafts of the agreement, and the three gentlemen had tea and a light repast before Darcy and Bingley headed out to look at Netherfield.

Darcy did not meet the rest of the Bennet family, as they were visiting the neighbors. Elizabeth had warned him that her mother was likely to be overwhelmingly vocal when she met him, and he was not certain if he was disappointed or relieved to have missed her.

The ride to Netherfield was short, as it was a mere three miles from Longbourn. Darcy and his friend met Mr. Phillips there and looked at the house and surrounding property.

"What do you think, Darcy? It seems to be in good condition."

"It does. I see no structural problems, and the house is old enough that it should have settled as much as it is going to. The property drains well and is well maintained."

"I think I shall take it, then."

"I think you should. I will come stay with you if you are opening the house soon. Elizabeth will probably wish to marry from Longbourn, and I do not want to be separated from her any longer than I must be."

"In that case, I will speak to the housekeeper as soon as I am done signing the lease and she may begin to hire staff. How long will Miss Elizabeth remain in London?"

"I hope to persuade her to not return until you move in here. I know that Miss Bennet will stay a bit longer, as will Miss Mary, but Elizabeth will want to begin planning the wedding, I am certain."

In short order, Bingley had the lease signed, and the gentlemen were on their way back to town.

Chapter 4

"Mr. Darcy to see you, ma'am." The maid curtseyed, then moved out of the way for Darcy to enter. It was the first time Elizabeth had seen him since he proposed two days previously. Her breath caught as she rose from her seat, Mary beside her, to see his handsome form enter the room. When he smiled, her heart began to race and a matching grin formed on her lips.

He bowed before her, taking her hand and bestowing a warm, lingering kiss on her fingers. Rising, his eyes were arrested by the emotion he saw in hers. They stood staring at each other for a long moment, until Lady Watts bustled into the room, calling out a greeting.

Mary laughed when the couple jumped apart. "I was beginning to wonder if you would ever again take notice of anyone in the room."

"I am sorry, dearest Mary, if we ignored you. We did not intend to."

"All is well, Miss Elizabeth," declared Lady Watts, "for is not incivility the very essence of love? Sadly, we cannot leave you alone together, but Mary and I will take ourselves here to the fireside, and you and your betrothed may speak together privately." Winking at Elizabeth, she took Mary's arm and escorted her across the room.

Darcy was quick to take advantage of the relative freedom they were granted, and helped Elizabeth seat herself on a settee, sitting as close beside her as he dared.

"You spoke to my father yesterday?" Elizabeth had been anxious about the visit. Her mother and youngest sisters were unpredictable in that, while they were uniformly loud and unchecked, one never knew precisely what would come out of their mouths. She could not bear for Darcy to think less of her due to their behavior. She was not nearly as concerned about her father's permission being given. She knew that she had sprinkled enough hints in her letters that he would not think twice to grant it.

"I did." Darcy resisted the urge to hold her hand. "He has granted us permission to marry and given us his blessing. We discussed the details of your settlement, as well. I shall take a copy of the rough draft to him once it is completed; I took my notes to my solicitor upon my return yesterday evening."

"That is good news! And ... my mother?"

"Was not at home. Neither were your sisters. Mr. Bennet said they were out for the morning, visiting. Bingley and I took tea with him and then met your Uncle Phillips at Netherfield."

Elizabeth's brows rose. "Oh? What did Mr. Bingley think of the place? I confess I was not certain he was serious about leasing it."

"There are several reasons behind his decision, I think. He is very much taken with your sister. He has planned and searched for months for an estate to lease, as he plans to purchase one at some point. And, he does not wish to see me have to take rooms at an inn when he can provide better accommodations."

"That is very kind of him. He seems to be a good friend to you."

"Bingley is the best of friends. He is, perhaps, too easily swayed by those around him, but he is generous, kind, and loyal, and I could not ask for more."

"I am happy to hear that he likes Jane, for I can tell by her behavior that she likes him, as well. Tell me about his habits, though." She blushed. "Forgive my impertinence. I know such a question is not proper to ask, but I am – we all are – protective of each other. We have no brother to look out for us, and so we have taken it upon ourselves to do it for each other. I do not wish to offend, but Jane has a tender heart, and I would not have it broken, if it were possible."

Darcy was taken aback at first by her question, but he admired that quality in her … that protectiveness over her sisters. "Bingley has fallen in and out of love many times, but it has generally been more because of the ladies than his own actions." He paused. "Well, let me amend that. On occasion, his sisters, in particular his younger sister, Caroline, have convinced him that this or that lady did not share his affections. I suspect that they did not care for the lady's position in society, given Caroline and Louisa's attitudes toward me and my fortune. However, most of the time, the ladies in question did not truly care for him, and he discovered it before it was too late. I will say this of Bingley, for all his amiability and eagerness to please, he can be quite shrewd in his dealings. My guess is that he inherited the trait from his father, who was an excellent man of business and who left Bingley with a large fortune."

"You are saying, then, that if my sister truly does esteem him, he will be able to discern the fact? And ... will he allow his sisters to dissuade him, if Jane is his choice?"

Darcy thought a moment, considering how best to answer. "I believe that, as long as Bingley can see your sister's affection for him, he will rely upon his own counsel. I found her to be almost supernaturally serene when we met, so I will trust your judgement of the matter. If he comes to me, with your permission, I will share with him what you have told me."

"Oh, yes, please do! I should not like to see my sister's happiness ruined through misconception."

Her betrothed echoed her sentiments, and their conversation moved on to other topics.

~~~***~~~
~~~

On the day of Elizabeth's departure from London, her family and the Darcys gathered at Arthur Place. She was to be escorted to Longbourn by her betrothed and his sister, as well as Charles Bingley and his family. The Hursts had returned to London so that Bingley's sister could serve as his hostess at Netherfield.

After much hugging and kissing and assurances of correspondence between Elizabeth and Georgiana, and Mary and the family, Darcy handed first his sister and then his future wife into his travelling coach before boarding it himself. They proceeded to Brook Street, where Bingley and the Hursts were waiting. In no time at all, the merry group was on its way.

They passed the time in quiet conversation. Except for Darcy and Georgiana, they were an outgoing bunch and before much time had passed, were speaking like old friends. The trip from London to Hertfordshire was a long one, however, and after the first stop, they found quiet pursuits such as reading and napping, in an effort to save their voices.

They arrived at Longbourn just after tea, having dropped Georgiana, Bingley, and his family off first at their estate. For the first time, Darcy experienced the whirlwind that was Mrs. Bennet. He was shocked at her poor manners and loud exclamations.

Elizabeth cringed every time her mother opened her mouth. She feared that Darcy would end their engagement, so haughty was his expression. She could tell he was offended. *He is probably wondering if he truly wishes to be a part of such a family.*

Darcy, however, was wishing he could take Elizabeth away from her home today instead of weeks from now. For every word Mrs. Bennet spoke in praise of him, she had three that were disparaging of her daughter, a fact that angered him beyond expression. When she tried to draw him into the conversation by asking his opinion, he firmly responded that he thought Elizabeth was everything wonderful and that, as her mother, Mrs. Bennet should be praising her to the skies. Not knowing what to say in response, the matron turned the conversation to other areas.

When the time came for him to leave, Elizabeth got him alone and expressed her worry. Darcy was quick to comfort her and assure her that ending their understanding was the furthest thing from his mind.

On the second day of her return to Hertfordshire, Elizabeth found herself and her sisters walking into Meryton to visit their aunt. Darcy was spending the morning with Bingley and would come to Longbourn for dinner. As they approached the Phillips' residence, Lydia called out a greeting to an officer, part of the militia unit quartered in the town for the winter, who was just across the way. He came across to greet the party with another man in tow. The officer, Lieutenant Denny, was just introducing his friend, one George Wickham, when Darcy and Bingley rode up the street.

Seeing the Bennet ladies, the gentlemen from Netherfield stopped to greet them. Bingley moved on, as he had business with the blacksmith that must be attended to right away. Mr. Wickham was trying to engage Elizabeth in conversation, which made her uneasy. Darcy, who had ignored the other men in favor of gazing upon his love, immediately saw the discomfort in her face. He began to look at the officer and his companion in order to determine the source of her distress when his attention was arrested by a visage he had hoped to never see again. In an instant, he was off his horse and by Elizabeth's side.

"Are you well, my love?"

The relief on her face was instant. "Yes, Fitzwilliam, I am. This gentleman was just making himself known to me." She refused to look back at the newcomer and therefore missed the paling of his skin and the flash of fear in his features.

"I see this." He took her hand as he spoke and tucked it under his elbow, holding it close. Turning away from her, he addressed the man. "Wickham. Fancy meeting you here. What is your purpose in visiting this village?"

"See here, Darcy, I have just as much right to walk these streets as you. Maybe more. I am signing up with the militia. I have funds to purchase a lieutenant's commission. I have to do something to make my way, since you refused to give me the living your father left me."

"You were compensated richly for the living and signed it away. Do not think you will get away with spreading that story here. Fitzwilliam is looking for you. I spared your life after our last encounter; I will not do it again. My advice to you is to leave town immediately, because before this day ends, I will have sent him an express giving him your location, and you know what that means. I will not have you trifle with any female in this town, not if I can prevent it."

Wickham had grown even more pale at the mention of Darcy's cousin. His bravado, however, had yet to desert him. He turned to Elizabeth. "I heard Darcy call you his love. Are you his mistress, then? He cannot be engaged to you; he is already betrothed to his cousin de Bourgh." He jumped back when Darcy reached for him, turning and running the other direction.

Elizabeth gasped at Wickham's words, turning her eyes to Darcy. "What is this?" she cried.

Darcy glared after the man running across the street, but dared not leave Elizabeth after what she had heard. He turned to her, grasping her hand in his when she would try to withdraw it from his arm. "I am not engaged to my cousin." He looked around them. "Is there a place of privacy where we can speak? I would not have this story overheard."

Elizabeth's eyes searched his face. "I am sure my aunt will let us use my uncle's study. Come, she lives here, and my sisters have just now entered."

She led him up the stairs and into the house. Her Aunt Philipps greeted her with a kiss and curtseyed to Darcy. As expected, she granted her permission for the couple to use her husband's study for a few minutes.

Elizabeth led her betrothed to the small, book-lined room and shut the door behind them. Once there, Darcy explained the whole of his acquaintance with Mr. Wickham, as well as the engagement that existed only in his Aunt Catherine's mind.

"Mr. Wickham convinced Georgiana that he was in love with her? How horrible! The poor girl!"

"She was inconsolable for weeks."

"How could someone who was so close to you as a child, and so favored by your father, despite his position as the son of Pemberley's steward, turn against the very family who supported him?"

"Wickham has shown tendencies toward profligacy since he was a child. My father never saw it, for it was only displayed when we were away from the house. Wickham's own father did his best to rein his son in, but Mrs. Wickham was a spendthrift, and since he spent more time with her than with his father, my childhood friend learned to want more than what he could afford. It grew much worse when we were at Eton. By the time we went on to Cambridge, I was forced to distance myself from him, though it was always me who cleaned up his messes and paid his debts.”

“Why did you not allow him to be exposed?”

“For my father’s sake. Papa was never the same after my mother passed away. He grew more and more ill. I was afraid he would not survive the shock of discovering that his favorite was not what he thought him to be, nor would he survive if scandal was attached to the Darcy name. Then, he passed away, just as I was finishing my studies. I had no reason to continue to ease Wickham’s path; I wanted to be done with him. So, when he told me he did not want to take the orders that were the condition of his receiving the living at Kympton, I was happy to give him monetary remuneration for it. I knew he should not be a clergyman.”

“And he went through three thousand pounds?”

“Four, and in less than two years.”

“And then he had the audacity to ask for more!”

“Yes.”

“Well.” Elizabeth was uncertain what else could be said about the man ... she could not in good conscience call him a gentleman ... that she had met today. She turned her thoughts to the other, more weighty matter. “And ... your cousin?”

Darcy sighed. This was even more difficult to explain, because it was positively mortifying. "My aunt, Lady Catherine de Bourgh, has stated, often and loudly, that my cousin Anne and I are formed for each other. She claims it to be the wish of my late mother that we marry. I do not know how my cousin feels about it, but I never had any intention of marrying her. Where I believe I have failed is that, instead of confronting my aunt with the truth, I simply ignored her. I should have made it plain long ago that I would not tie myself to my cousin."

Elizabeth nodded, taking the information in and considering it. "Is there a particular reason you did not wish to marry her? She is far higher in consequence than I, and likely has a handsome fortune."

"That is true, on both counts. However, aside from the simple fact that I do not love my cousin and cannot think of her in the position of my wife, Anne has nothing to recommend her. She is of a sickly constitution, and has never learned the accomplishments that a gentlewoman of our sphere should. She has no conversation and her countenance is perpetually sour. My aunt declares that Anne is the image of my mother, but I do not see the resemblance. My mother was delicate, but she enjoyed a good turn about the gardens and had a healthy glow to her skin. My cousin does not."

"You prefer a lady who enjoys her exercise?"

Darcy took a step closer. "Indeed, I do, and one who reads and is capable of intelligent discussion."

"You are not engaged to her, then, and have no desire to be?"

"No and no. I only wish to marry you."

"What is your aunt going to say when she learns of our engagement?"

"I care not. I do not answer to Lady Catherine, nor to her brother, the earl. I am my own man."

"What does your uncle say about it?"

"I do not know; I have not spoken to him. I do, however, expect a letter soon. I wrote to him the other day announcing my engagement and removal to Hertfordshire. I also wrote to Lady Catherine."

Elizabeth considered what he said. "Very well. I love you and do not wish to give you up. If you are certain that your relatives cannot separate us, then I will put them out of my mind."

Darcy pulled her into his arms. "I am certain." Before he could kiss Elizabeth, as he dearly wished to, there came a knock on the door and the sound of her sister, Kitty, calling for them. They pulled away from one another with looks of regret.

The door opened and Kitty stuck her head in. "Lizzy, are you coming? Aunt is ready to serve the tea!"

"We are right behind you. Thank you for coming to get us."

"Think nothing of it, but hurry! I am hungry!"

~~~***~~~

The first days of Darcy's visit to Hertford-shire were filled with dinners and teas celebrating his engagement to Elizabeth. Darcy, who was never comfortable with strangers, thought it a trial, though he greatly enjoyed watching Elizabeth flit around the room, speaking with everyone and lighting up the place with her smile. Through her presence, he found himself able to easily bear the intrusive inquiries of the neighborhood into his life.

The week after their arrival, there was a ball scheduled at the Assembly Hall. The ladies that inhabited Longbourn were mad with glee, for all of them who were in residence loved to dance. They spent the entire week preparing, remaking gowns and practicing the steps. Darcy, Bingley, and even Mr. Bennet were called upon to assist the ladies with the latter. Finally, the night of the dance arrived.

Darcy assisted his betrothed out of the carriage, escorting her inside while Mr. Bennet handed the rest of the family down.

"Fitzwilliam, where is Mr. Bingley? I thought he might come with you."

"Ah, Bingley rode back to town today." Darcy's smirk intrigued Elizabeth.

"He did? Why?"
~~~

"Because, as he put it ..." Here Darcy changed his voice to one slightly higher that closely matched Bingley's tone. "I long for Miss Bennet's company far too much to be easy attending an assembly without her. I would much rather be by her side."

Elizabeth squeezed his arm as she laughed. "Oh, do tell! I am so happy to hear that. Jane will be delighted to see him."

"I rather expect to hear of an engagement between the two of them soon."

"Oh, I hope so! Two more closely matched people I have never seen. They are both so easygoing!"

"Yes, and if they do marry, they will likely be taken in by their servants and not have the heart to do anything about it."

Rosings Park, Kent

Lady Catherine de Bourgh accepted the post from her butler with a stiff nod. Shuffling through the pile, she saw that she had received a letter from her favorite nephew. It was rare for him to write, and so, dropping the rest of the mail, she broke the seal and swiftly unfolded the missive. She anticipated a clear statement of his intent to set a wedding date with her daughter. She was, however, angered to read that he had engaged himself to someone else.

Bennet? She thought to herself. *Bennet?? I know of no family by that name.* She rang the bell to call the butler back as she reread the letter.

"My lady?"

"Order my coach readied for a trip to ..." She looked at the missive again. "Hertford-shire. We shall leave tomorrow morning. I will require a boy to deliver instructions to the inns between here and town, for I will be stopping there for the night. Oh, and go to the library and find my copy of Debrett's and bring it here."

"Yes, ma'am." The servant bowed before turning to complete his assignments. Lady Catherine immediately sat down to write letters of her own, arranging for horses and breaks at inns along the way, and for her townhouse to be opened for her use and that of her daughter.

"Mama, what are you doing? The servants seem to be running about in a frenzy. Mrs. Jenkinson has ordered my maid to pack a trunk for me. Are we going somewhere?" Anne de Bourgh was made uneasy at the thought of travelling. It was not something she and her mother did often, and it generally meant a great deal of discomfort. Anne was a lady who liked her comforts.

"We are indeed going somewhere. I received a letter from Darcy in today's post. It seems he has engaged himself to someone. Someone who obviously is not you."

"Really?" Anne's relief in this news displayed itself in a delighted smile. She had no desire to marry anyone, especially not her cousin. He was a good looking gentleman, solid and well-built in all the right places, but he was also frighteningly tall and large. She always tried to make herself as small as possible so as to escape his notice when he visited. He never disagreed with her mother about the supposed betrothal between them, and Anne had taken that to mean he would eventually get around to asking. She hated to disappoint anyone, and hated more to be at odds with her mother, but she would have turned him down. Every Easter for years she had marshalled the arguments she would use with him and with her mother for her refusal, because she knew it would take all of her strength and energy to stand her ground.

As quickly as her reaction showed on her face, Anne masked it. It would not do for her mother to see it. She would save her energy for later, when she would have to support Darcy's decision.

The next morning, as soon as Anne had broken her fast, she and her mother boarded the coach. The trip was short, only half a day's journey, but Anne's delicate health required that they stop for the night in London and leave again the next morning.

So it was that, two days after she received Darcy's letter, Lady Catherine and her daughter entered the village of Meryton. Her instructions to her coachman were to find Longbourn, for that was the name of the estate she had found in the peerage register. Her shock had been great to discover the connection to the aristocracy that the Bennet family could claim. It was unexpected; however, her daughter still retained a prior claim to Darcy. She could not let this supposed engagement stand. She held the strap as her coachman brought the equipage to a stop. Out the window, she could see three young ladies about to enter what appeared to be a seamstress' shop.

"Good day, Miss!"

All three Bennet daughters turned at the sound of the coach stopping and the driver hailing someone. Realizing he was calling to them, Elizabeth stepped forward. "Good afternoon, sir!"

"Could you tell me where to find an estate called Longbourn? The Bennet family?"

Taken aback, Elizabeth glanced at Kitty and Lydia, who had moved to stand at her left side, and then back to the coachman. Before she could utter a word, Lydia spoke, pointing her finger toward the road.

"Why, Longbourn is our home. It is just down the way here."

The driver's face showed surprise. "You are Bennets? All of you?"

"We are." Kitty giggled at the man's look.

Turning to the groom beside him, the driver spoke. "Get on down there and tell the mistress we have found some Bennets."

"Yes, sir."

Both Lady Catherine and Anne had been listening to the exchange. Anne had shrunk down in her seat as far as she dared as the door opened.

"Ma'am? These here ladies are Bennets."

Elizabeth was confused, as were her sisters. She could see from the design of the carriage that it did not belong to anyone she knew. Suddenly, a voice floated out, harsh and angry.

"Which one of you is Miss Elizabeth Bennet?"

Elizabeth took one step forward. "I am."

"Come in here so that I may speak to you."

Now, Elizabeth was not at all worldly, but neither was she stupid. "Thank you for asking, but I would rather not. We have not been introduced, and I do not enter the carriages of strangers. You may present yourself to my father at Longbourn. I will give your coachman directions. Good day, madam."

Elizabeth looked up to the coachman as Lady Catherine railed at her, and explained to him how to find the estate. She then gathered her sisters and entered the shop without looking back.

Lady Catherine was left sputtering, with no method of releasing her anger. Anne had watched the entire proceedings with delight. Why, the lady had treated her mother as though she were as common as a tree. Not many people attempted that, much less got away with it, so Anne was enjoying it while it lasted. She hid her laugh behind her hand, turning her head to the window.

Chapter 5

For all that Elizabeth was done with the imperious woman in the elegant carriage, that woman was by no means done with her. Lady Catherine's anger was at full boil, and when the step was let down in front of Longbourn's door, she marched up the steps and knocked herself, not waiting for her servant.

"I am Lady Catherine de Bourgh. I demand to see Mr. Bennet immediately."

Mrs. Hill, Longbourn's housekeeper, jumped at the visitor's tone. She curtseyed, opening the door wider. "Please come in. He is in his book room. If you will wait here, I will tell him you wish to speak with him. He has another guest with him right now."

Lady Catherine, however, was not one to consent to cooling her heels in anyone's hallway, and followed the servant to a wood-panelled door all the way at the end of the hall. When the door opened, Lady Catherine pushed past Mrs. Hill before the housekeeper could announce her. Her anger only grew to see her nephew in the room with an older gentleman who she knew must be the one she had come to see.

Rising at her entrance, the gentlemen both bowed to her. Darcy spoke before she could get a word out. "Lady Catherine, it is a surprise to see you here."

Her eyes narrowed. "Why should it be a surprise? Surely you knew when you sent your letter that I would respond?"

"Well, yes, I did, but I expected a reply in kind, not for you to venture forth from Kent to congratulate me in person."

"Congratulate you? Why would I congratulate you? I see no reason for it, unless you break this farce of an engagement."

"I have no intentions of ending my engagement, Aunt." Darcy's tone was severe, but the words were quietly spoken.

"You must. You are engaged to my daughter, and have been since your infancy. It was the greatest wish of your mother for the two of you to join together. For you to reject her now is cruelty in its highest form, for Anne and for the young woman to whom you have proposed. Both will be ridiculed, my daughter for being jilted and Miss Bennet for reaching above her station. Your friends will reject you, and she will never be admitted to society."

"Funny how my mother never told me about any understanding she made with you. Nor did my father. Ever. In his effects were no marriage contracts between Anne and me, no settlement articles." Darcy's voice became hard as flint. "Any engagement between myself and my cousin was a mere figment of your imagination, Lady Catherine. I should have spoken to you about it years ago, and I apologize to you for that failure. However, my friends and anyone else who actually cares about me will neither ridicule me nor reject me, or my wife, whoever she may be. Those who love me best will desire my happiness and will embrace the one who makes me so." He stepped closer to her before he continued. "Any rejection will come about as a result of the machinations and slander of those who do not care for me, and will be met with the excision of those people from our lives. Do I make myself clear, Aunt?"

For a full minute, the great woman was speechless, having never expected such harsh words from her favorite nephew, delivered in such a hard manner. When words did return to her, they spewed forth in language so very abusive, especially of Elizabeth, that Darcy was hard pressed not to grab her and toss her out the window. Thankfully, Mr. Bennet intervened, ringing for Mrs. Hill, who had already heard enough of the din through the door to summon the footman along with the grooms from the stables. The servants quietly entered the room, taking up positions all around Lady Catherine.

"Enough!" Mr. Bennet roared the word in a tone not heard in the house in at least a decade. Pointing at his future son-in-law's aunt, he informed her in no uncertain terms that he would not tolerate abuse of his family from anyone and that she had the choice to leave on her own or to be escorted out.

His words startled her into awareness of her surroundings and, finally seeing the gathered men edging closer to her, she raised her nose in the air, turned around, and exited the room. She muttered all the way to the door, leaving no one in doubt of her feelings.

Finally, the house was quiet again. Darcy, still red with rage, took a deep breath. Turning away from the door and facing his betrothed's father, he spoke. "I apologize for my aunt, sir. She had no right to come here to accost anyone, and even less to denigrate Miss Elizabeth."

Mr. Bennet sighed, still angry himself, but drained from the emotion. "Thank you, but the apology should come from her. Apparently, being a peer does not guarantee proper behavior in a person."

"No, indeed, it does not, which is why my father taught my sister and myself to judge people on their actions and not their position in society. Never have I been more grateful for that lesson."

Bennet nodded. That was something he wished more people had learned. "Well, I do not know about you, but I require a drink after all that. Would you like one?"

Darcy chuckled. "I believe that to be a fine idea, sir."

~~~***~~~

George Wickham eased himself away from the window looking into Longbourn's book
~~~

room, fading into the shadows of the large oaks that shaded the house. He had spent the days since his confrontation with Darcy mostly in hiding, following his childhood friend around and monitoring his habits. It did not take him long to figure out that Darcy was truly enamored of the Bennet girl and to begin trailing her, as well.

When he could, Wickham spent time in the local inn's taproom, listening to the gossip of the town. That was where he received confirmation of the engagement between Darcy and Elizabeth. Now, he had discovered that Darcy's family, part of it anyway, was opposed to the match.

Wickham wanted revenge, and now he knew just how to accomplish it. He returned to the inn for a meal, and then ventured into the night to the abandoned outbuilding he had found on the other side of Longbourn. Keeping to himself, he planned out every detail. Looking around his hiding place, he thought that it would serve his needs well. He pulled an old letter and a small pencil out of his pocket and made a list of items to purchase on the morrow. For safety's sake, he would ride out to the next town to buy them. He did not intend to be caught, but it was always better to be safe than sorry. Tucking his paper and pencil back where he found it, Wickham lay back on the pile of rags he was using for a bed and reflected on the Darcys, in particular the current master of Pemberley.

Wickham had always been jealous of Fitzwilliam Darcy. The heir to Pemberley could do no wrong, it seemed, always receiving preferred treatment and praise for every accomplishment. Wickham received praise, as well, but his mother's words about how little they had and how much more they needed rang in his ears. His father was a hard-working man, and well-respected on the estate. On some level, Wickham knew that his mother spent every farthing her husband earned, but as he was more often with her than with his father, it was her opinion that formed his. So, even though Wickham was not the heir to the great estate, he never learned to be happy with his lot in life and, once his mother passed away, his envy of young Darcy grew and he began to rebel.

He started out with small things; leaving stall doors unlatched after riding, being too rough in his play, and sending a greased pig into the kitchens. When he was sent to Eton along with Darcy and met more young men, he began to be drawn to the ones who did not follow the rules. His tricks became meaner and had more of a tormenting quality to them. And, they were not aimed solely at Darcy any longer. By the time they entered Cambridge, Wickham was carousing with peers, involved in gambling and drinking and debauchery of all kinds. He often impersonated his godfather's son. His group of friends thought this was a hoot. Darcy was reserved and quiet. He excelled in both sports and academics, though he preferred solitary pursuits such as reading and riding. Few of the other boys understood his serious and studious nature.

Then came the deaths of Darcy's father and his own and the fiasco that was his bequest in the elder Darcy's will. Wickham's attempted elopement with Georgiana Darcy was his first effort at revenge. If not for the empty-headed chit's urge to tell her brother all the details, it would have worked. He would have had a pretty, obedient young woman in his bed, un-limited access to one of the finest estates in all England, and thirty thousand pounds in his hand. He shook his head at the memory. *Too bad that did not work out. This scheme will, though. It is perfect.*

Two Days Later ...

Elizabeth strode with sure steps to the fence that marked the border between her father's estate and the first of the tenant hous-es, on the other side of Longbourn from Neth-erfield. She planned today to walk along that fence to the creek and then follow the water for a bit before going home. She was expected to visit Darcy and Georgiana later today at Bingley's estate, but she required the respite that sunshine and exercise provided before she returned to the chaos of Longbourn and her mother's tactless, shrill pronouncements and unsolicited advice.

Having just made the turn from the fence line to the creek, Elizabeth heard a noise in the woods nearby. She stopped for a moment, the hairs on the back of her neck standing up and a feeling of apprehension overtaking her. She listened intently, hoping to determine what had made the unusual sound, but all was quiet. Shaking herself, she put the thought away, chuckling silently at her missish reaction. Turning back to the path that ran along the small stream, she began walking once again.

Suddenly, she heard quick steps behind her and before she could turn around, an arm was around her waist and a hand clamped over her mouth. Frozen for a few seconds in shock, Elizabeth did not react immediately, but when she felt herself pulled back tightly against a person's body, she began to fight. She kicked at her attacker, and when he grunted in pain, she was able to determine that it was a man. Continuing to use her legs and feet, as well as her arms and hands, she fought to be free, but he was too strong. She scratched at his hands and face between jabs into his ribs with her elbows as he dragged her backward to the tree line. Then, the world went dark.

Wickham cursed as Elizabeth fought him with all she had, ordering her to desist. She ignored him, and her wriggling made it more difficult for him to get her out of sight. Once she scratched his face, he had had enough. Removing his arm from her waist, he struck her, and she slumped to the ground. Not checking the state of her health, he picked her back up, this time throwing her over his shoulder.

He walked steadily toward his destination, keeping to the trees as much as possible, and skirting the farms as best he could. He stopped twice to rest, unceremoniously dropping his prisoner to the ground. The first time, he tied her hands behind her back and her legs and knees together with rope he had hidden at the site. He tied an extra cravat he had in his pocket around her mouth. It would not do for her to awaken and scream. He could not be found out before he got far away from Meryton.

Finally, he arrived at the abandoned building he had designated as his base of operations. Once more, he dropped his cargo, this time on the dirt floor of the shed. Elizabeth, who had awakened on the second leg of the trip and had wiggled around trying to get away until he had slapped her bottom and told her to behave, grunted in pain before looking around the room.

"Do not think that you will escape. It will not be possible. You are here as my revenge on Darcy, my retribution for taking my inheritance and his sister and her dowry from me. You will remain in this cabin, just as you are, until someone finds you. It could be hours, days, or even weeks, before you are discovered, and Darcy will be in agony. His betrothed, lost to him; I know that it will cause him pain. I have seen the two of you together. I see the affection he has for you. I know him well … he would not offer for you if he did not love you, nor would he tolerate your family. You are important to him. He has taken from me things that were important to me, and now I am returning the favor." Wickham tipped his hat to her. "Good day, Miss Elizabeth." With that, he turned and exited the building, shutting the door behind him.

Elizabeth was horrified. She had known already that Wickham's character was less than stellar. That he would stoop to kidnapping was unfathomable. As her mind raced through the facts and the possibilities, she became distraught. No one knew where she was or when she had left. She did not even know where she was! Worse, she had no way of escaping and making her way to help. There was no furniture in the room at all, and the manner in which Wickham had tied her made it impossible for her to walk, even if she could manage to stand.

Her stomach grumbled, reminding her that she had not yet broken her fast. That was another disheartening thing. There was neither food nor water available to her. She had read enough to know that people did not survive long without them.

Elizabeth was, however, not one to give up easily. She tried repeatedly over the course of the day to find a way to escape her bindings. She wiggled herself all over the room, but the walls, though old, were well-constructed and the nails still firmly embedded in them, at least the ones she could reach. By the time the light began to dim, she was exhausted and hungrier and thirstier than she had ever been. She slept fitfully, her dreams filled with nightmares of what had happened and what might soon occur.

The first shafts of sunlight woke her the next morning, shining through cracks in the wooden walls. Her mouth dry and her stomach hurting, she tried once more to find a way out. She was, however, much weaker, and before long, she stilled, remaining where she was. She began to move in and out of consciousness, dreaming of Darcy and of her family between periods of blackness.

Chapter 6

Darcy sat in the library at Netherfield attending to his correspondence. His pen moved steadily across the page, only stopping to dip into the inkpot, and his mouth moved as he wrote. His focus was centered on his letters, because he hoped to have them completed before his beloved arrived from Longbourn. He was so engrossed in his work that he did not hear his sister enter the room and take a seat on a nearby settee.

Georgiana, seeing that her brother was absorbed in his writing, did not disturb him at first. She opened her book, keeping one eye on the tome and one on Darcy. Finally, he folded the letter and addressed it, and she took the opportunity to attract his attention.

"Fitzwilliam," she began, glancing at the clock on the mantel. "Was Miss Elizabeth not supposed to be here by now?"

Darcy pulled his watch out of his pocket, checking it against the clock. "She was." His brows came together in a frown. "I wonder where she is?" He looked up and out the window, gathering his thoughts and ordering them, examining facts and discarding speculations. Finally, he came to a conclusion, which he shared with the patiently waiting Georgiana. "Let me send a note to Longbourn. I cannot imagine what would have kept her from coming, but perhaps there was an emergency."

His sister watched as he wrote on another piece of paper, rising to ring the bell for him. "I hope all is well. Would she not have sent a note of her own if she could not come? Maybe she is just late."

Darcy shook his head. "No, Elizabeth is never late, and she would have at least sent a servant to inform us if she had been prevented from coming."

Just then, the footman entered the library. Darcy handed him the missive, with instructions to send a boy with it to Longbourn and that he should wait for a response. Before the man could turn to go, Darcy asked him to send Mrs. Nichols in. Surely Bingley's housekeeper would know if a verbal message had been delivered. She was well-organized and nothing escaped her notice.

"You asked to see me, Mr. Darcy?"

"I did. Thank you for responding so promptly. Can you tell me if a servant has been here from Longbourn with any kind of message?"

"Oh, no, sir. We have not seen anyone here today at all, beyond the pair of you and the Hursts. I would have had it passed on to you immediately, in any case. Were you expecting one?"

"No, not expecting ..." Darcy paused. *I cannot shake a feeling of apprehension. I hope there is nothing wrong, and yet I cannot let go of this fear.* He shook himself and then dismissed the housekeeper, then forced himself to make small talk with Georgiana while they waited for a response from Longbourn.

He had just begun pacing the library in impatience when Mrs. Nichols entered the room once more, bearing a piece of paper. She handed it to Darcy, who paled upon opening it.

"Fitzwilliam, what is the matter?"

Darcy opened his mouth to reply to Georgiana's question when a footman entered with another missive, handing it immediately to Darcy and exiting the room. Darcy instantly recognized the handwriting on the envelope as that of his former friend. His heart in his mouth, he swallowed an oath as he opened it and read the contents.

Darcy,

You had it all and took what was mine. Now I have taken what is yours. Miss Elizabeth is alive. For now. Good luck finding her.

W.

"What does it say? Tell me, Fitzwilliam!" Georgiana had never seen her brother with that look on his face, a combination of anger and fear.

Darcy's gaze focused on his sister. As much as he hated to bring that blackguard's name up to her again, he could not leave her in the dark about it. "Wickham has taken Elizabeth, I know not where." At Georgiana's gasp, Darcy tried to reassure her. "We will find her. All will be well."

Her eyes filling with tears at the thought of the lady she already considered a sister being in the clutches of a man such as George Wickham, she begged Darcy to let her help. "What can I do to assist? I could not bear to sit here doing nothing."

"For now, just pray. I need to question the servants and ride to Longbourn to speak to Mr. Bennet. His note says that Elizabeth left the house before breaking her fast, probably around nine o'clock but that he could not say for certain, and that she generally only stays out for an hour. When she did not return to eat with them, they assumed she came here."

"Instead, Wickham kidnapped her. Poor Lizzy! Oh, poor Mary, when she hears, she will be so worried!"

Darcy walked over and pulled the bell. When the footman appeared, he demanded to know who had delivered the letter from Wickham.

"'Twas a local boy, sir. One of the black-smith's younger sons."

"When was it delivered? Did you give it to me immediately?"

"Yes, sir. He delivered it to the front door, and I walked straight down the hall to give it to you. Made no extra stops."

"Very good. You are dismissed. Oh, wait!" He paused for a moment as the servant stopped and turned back. "Have my horse saddled. I need to ride to Longbourn immediately."

"Yes, sir." Nodding, he turned once more and hurried to give the stables the message.

"Georgiana, I want you to stay in your rooms while I am gone. Lock the door and let no one in, not even your maid. I do not trust that Wickham will not attempt something with you, and use someone from the household to do it. I will tell Hurst before I leave that I have given you those orders."

"I will do as you say. Please bring Lizzy home quickly." Kissing his cheek, she swiftly exited the library and took herself up the stairs, locking herself in her chambers.

Once Darcy had informed the Hursts, who were settled in the drawing room for the afternoon, he strode out the door and mounted his waiting stallion. Within minutes, he was being granted entrance to Longbourn.

~~~***~~~

Darcy and Mr. Bennet, after a brief consultation, came to the conclusion that they should make sure Wickham did not take Elizabeth to London. They needed to know where to begin the search. By Darcy's estimation, she had been gone for seven hours.

With only a short period of daylight left, he commissioned the fastest of Netherfield's grooms, one whom he had asked to attend him to Longbourn, to ride first into Meryton to check the coach stop there and then on to the next one. He was to report back as soon as
~~~

possible. The gentlemen felt that Wickham would have entered the coach at one of those two stops. Travelling with a lady, especially one as spirited and stubborn as Elizabeth could be when angered, would not be conducive to the speed and unremarkable demeanor that he needed to maintain to get away.

While the groom was gone, Darcy and Bennet formed a plan to search the area, in case it was needed. They called in the steward, who was able to help them identify possible hiding places.

It was full dark by the time the groom returned with news that no couples had entered coaches at either stop. The gentlemen were relieved to hear that their search would be a local one. The servant, however, had more to share with them.

"I heard an interesting fact in Meryton, though, that might be meaningful to you." He waited for nods indicating permission to speak further, continuing his tale upon receiving them. "I recall hearing, Mr. Darcy, that you chased off a gentleman named Wickham. He left the county, so I was told, but he was seen late this morning entering the coach. The innkeeper's wife told me he was looking all around, as though someone was after him. She said he has not been gone at all, but has been coming in to drink in the evenings, and to gamble a bit."

"Which stop was this?" Darcy's visage was pale at the thought that Wickham had remained nearby.

"The Meryton stop, sir."

Darcy cursed, turning to face the window. Bennet dismissed the groom before addressing his companion. "So it seems Mr. Wickham has been watching you."

"And Elizabeth, is my guess. If he has hurt her, I swear I will tear this country apart looking for him."

"It is too late to begin the search. We have already checked this house and the stables and outbuildings. You are welcome to spend the night here."

"Thank you, but my sister is locked in her chambers awaiting word from me. I will return to Netherfield, but will be back at first light. I will set the servants there to searching the house and grounds before I ride over here."

"Very good." Bennet put his hand on Darcy's shoulder and squeezed. "We will find her, and she will be well. We must cling to that."

Darcy nodded, giving Bennet a small smile, before striding out of the book room.

~~~***~~~

Darcy was back just as dawn broke the next morning. He had slept very little, worry over his beloved and anger at his childhood friend having eaten at him. He and Bennet
~~~

hastily ingested a quick meal before addressing the gathered gentry, servants, and tenants
of the local estates. Word had spread of Miss
Elizabeth's disappearance, and there were
many who were eager to help find her.

They searched the entire day, starting with
the farms attached to Longbourn and working
their way outward. Every building they found
was inspected, every attic, every hayloft, every
cellar. Darcy was tireless, pushing himself
and the men with him. Eventually, though,
darkness once again enveloped the land and
Elizabeth remained missing.

Darcy returned to his rooms at Netherfield,
disheartened and fearful. His sleep was even
more disturbed than it had been the previous
night. For every hour Elizabeth remained
missing, the hope for her good health – her
life, even – grew smaller. At dawn the next
day, he was once again knocking on Longbourn's door.

The sun was low in the sky when the men
of the neighborhood, after searching as far as
they thought a man could go when dragging
an unwilling woman behind him, gathered in
a field on the far side of the Bennet estate. All
were exhausted, and many had given up hope
that she would ever be found.

Two boys taking part in the search decided
to rest for a bit in a clump of trees nearby.
First hacking at the tall weeds to make a
path, one sat beneath a tree while the other

walked further in to relieve himself. With one hand on a tree and the other aiming his stream away from his feet, the second boy looked around. His attention was arrested by a path of bent weeds and broken branches amongst the thick trees and brush. Upon finishing his ablutions, he followed the trail, at the end finding a building he had never known was there. He pushed the door open and gasped to see a young lady, bound up and unconscious. He turned and ran, past his friend, to Mr. Bennet and the rich nob that was staying at Netherfield.

"I found her!"

At the boy's words, Darcy was off his horse and running after him. Bennet and the rest of the men followed.

Rushing into the hidden cabin, Darcy was both elated and heartbroken to find his betrothed. "Elizabeth!" He knelt at her side, feeling for a pulse in her neck as he reached with his other hand for the pocket knife he kept in his coat. Men began to fill the room, some helping Darcy untie her and others setting to work making a litter with which to carry her out.

Bennet lowered himself on the other side of his daughter. "Is she alive?"

"Yes, but barely," Darcy replied. He looked around the small space. "He left her here, tied up and with no food or water, for days. Days! He knows as well as anyone that she could have died here. She may yet-" He choked on the words, tears coming to his eyes. He gripped her hand as he worked to control his emotions. "Please, Elizabeth, wake up. Do not leave me," he whispered.

Bennet spoke. "Does she have any injuries?"

"I do not know. We need to check before we move her." They set about feeling her limbs and body. When they found nothing to indicate a break, they rolled her from her side onto her back. Darcy growled at the sight of her bruised face, but he continued to check her for further injury. He was relieved to find nothing else beyond rope burns around her wrists. "I will kill him for this."

"And leave my daughter a widow when you are caught and hanged? I do not think so. We will find him and deal with him, but for now, we must focus on Elizabeth."

Darcy nodded, gathering his intended in his arms. He whispered in her ear, "Please, my darling, come back to me. Do not leave me." He kissed her ear and her cheek, and then, so very softly, her lips. "I love you."

The litter was ready for use and so, reluctantly, Darcy laid Elizabeth down on it, covering her with his coat. He insisted on carrying one corner of it and helping walk her out. She was far too precious to entrust to people he did not know.

It was a long, slow walk back to Longbourn and there were frequent stops to allow the men to take turns on the litter. Never once did

Elizabeth stir, and fear gripped every man among them that she would not survive.

Upon reaching the manor, the local apothecary was set up to receive her in her bedchamber, having been summoned as soon as Elizabeth was found. Darcy gathered her up and carried her in himself, leaving only at the insistence of the housekeeper and the man of medicine. He stationed himself outside her door, where he could keep watch on her progress. Soon, Mr. Bennet joined him. Suddenly, the door opened and the housekeeper stuck her head out. "She is waking!"

Darcy rushed to her bed, sitting on the edge and holding her hand. "Elizabeth?" Joy filled him when her head turned toward him and her eyes opened.

"Fitzwilliam," she croaked.

He kissed her hand. "I love you."

"Love ... you ..."

The apothecary spoke. "She needs water. I have read of people who died as a result of not drinking enough liquids. Mrs. Hill has gone down to fetch broth, but we also need to give her sips of water, slowly but often."

Darcy nodded as he changed his position on the bed. Lifting her up, he leaned Elizabeth against his chest. Bennet handed him a glass of water, and he coaxed her to drink, pulling it away after just a little bit. "Not too much, my love. Let that settle and I will give you more."

Elizabeth managed to stay awake long enough to take half the water in the glass and a small amount of broth. Darcy and her father took turns with the apothecary and Mrs. Hill, watching her for signs of fever and encouraging her to take water whenever she awakened, even if it was for only a few minutes. When she survived the night, her caretakers were elated, and the news was relayed to her mother and youngest sisters, who had been confined to their rooms once Elizabeth had been found. Mr. Bennet had decided that theatrics were not needed in the sickroom and that was all the three women were capable of.

London, late the next day

Colonel Richard Fitzwilliam settled into a chair in his quarters. His batman had handed him a letter upon his return to the barracks, saying it had arrived only minutes before. Seeing the return address and recalling that his Darcy cousins were currently staying with Darcy's friend, Bingley, he snapped the seal and unfolded the letter. Expecting it to be a simple recount of their days in the country, he was unprepared for the contents.

Leaping from his seat, he read the note again, his shock giving way to anger. He began to pace as his mind, with the precision that had gained him acclaim for his strategies in battle, plotted steps to avenge Darcy and his betrothed. After examining his plan from all angles, he sat down to write two letters. One was to a former comrade who made his money now by conducting investigations. The other was to his cousin.

Darcy,

I am without words. My anger knows no bounds. That your innocent betrothed should be left to die in such a manner horrifies and enrages me. I am relieved to hear that she is awake and on the path to recovery, and that the cur did not injure her further.

I know that you are not in a position to take care of this situation. You are rightly where you belong, with your Elizabeth. Be assured that I will, with all due diligence, address it as swiftly as I can manage and in as discreet a manner as possible. You should know by now that I am well able to arrange matters to suit me, and with no repercussions.

Give my love to both Georgiana and Miss Bennet. I have never been more eager to have her join the family.

Yours,

RF

~~~***~~~

Three days after Elizabeth awoke, Jane and Mary Bennet returned home, accompanied by
~~~

Mr. Bingley and Lord and Lady Watts. The young ladies rushed to their sister's side, with Jane taking over nursing duties from the housekeeper. She spent much of her time while at Elizabeth's bedside talking, sharing news and stories of her time in London. Mary, after sitting with Elizabeth for a while and holding her hand, retreated down the stairs.

Jane's relief that Elizabeth was recovering added to her excitement over her betrothal. "You must get well, dear sister, for I require that you stand up with me. Mr. Bingley has asked me to marry him, and I said yes. I am so happy! Perhaps we might have a double wedding? What do you say?"

Darcy and Bingley watched from the doorway. "She is happy, my friend. Congratulations. We shall be brothers."

Bingley grinned. "We shall. You are fortunate in that, are you not?"

Darcy laughed. "Indeed, I am. Fortunate on all fronts, I believe." He gazed at Elizabeth, who still slept most of the time but had regained some color and strength.

"Have you found Wickham yet? I knew he was a scoundrel but never imagined he would do something so heinous."

"No, I have not. I have hired investigators, though, and have alerted my cousin to be on the lookout for him."

"Ah, if I remember correctly, Wickham is very much afraid of the good colonel. What did Fitzwilliam say about the matter?"

"Not much, just that he would like an introduction to Elizabeth as soon as possible and that he knew if Lady Catherine described her as common and inappropriate that she must be a diamond of the first water. His anger was clear, however. Elizabeth is an innocent, just one of a long line of them, of course, but after the last incident, this one makes it clear that Wickham's behavior is becoming worse and worse. If I know Fitzwilliam, he believes the miscreant must be stopped and he is just the man to do it. That army training and his service on the battlefield have made him fierce. Wickham is wise to fear him. My cousin will find him, no matter how long it takes, and it will not go well, not for Wickham, at any rate."

"And in the meantime?"

"My focus, for now, remains on Elizabeth and getting her well. Georgiana has been asking to visit and help with the nursing duties. Now that Mary is here and my betrothed seems to be on the mend, I will allow it. She has always wanted a sister, and watching Jane and Mary serve theirs will teach Georgiana well."

The gentlemen moved out of the doorway as Mrs. Hill bustled past them, giving them a look that could only mean disapproval.

"She does not approve of us seeing Miss Elizabeth in her chambers?"

Darcy chuckled. "No, she does not. It does not matter a bit to her that Elizabeth is covered to her chin and that her sister sits with her. Gentlemen do not belong in a lady's bedchamber before they are wed. Come, Bennet had the settee in the hallway brought up for my comfort. Let us make use of it."

<h1 style="text-align:center">Chapter 7</h1>

It took Elizabeth a full week to recover her strength enough to leave her room. The apothecary insisted that she slowly increase the amount of food she consumed, and allowed her only broth for the first few days. He looked in on her daily, and was happy to report to her father and betrothed that she was making good progress. The day she stepped into the hall for the first time and felt Darcy's waiting arms wrap around her felt like the best day of her life.

"I love you, Fitzwilliam," she murmured into his waistcoat.

"And I, you, my love." Darcy tightened his hold. "You must promise not to frighten me that way again." His voice became imperious. "You will take a footman with you every time you leave the house. Never again will you be left unprotected."

For once in her life, Elizabeth was happy with that sort of demand. "I will, even if I only go to the gardens." She began to cry. "It was awful, Fitzwilliam, and I never wish to experience anything similar again. I tried to get out, I truly did, but there was nothing I could do. I could not stand and walk, and I could not find any way to get the bindings off."

Darcy picked her up and moved to the settee, sitting down with her in his lap. He held her while she cried, rubbing his hand over her back to comfort her. "Shhh, all is well, my love. I know that you tried. There was evidence of it on your gown and on the floor. I am so sorry that I did not find you sooner. Would that I could have spared you some of the horror!" Tears filled his own eyes as he shared with her his feelings of helplessness and pain at her disappearance. "I promise you, my love, that I will do everything in my power to keep you safe for the rest of your life. You are my heart; without you, I am a lost soul."

Darcy lifted Elizabeth's tear-stained face with his finger under her chin. He searched her eyes, looking for permission and assurance, and, finding both, lowered his lips to hers. They kissed for a long minute, giving and taking reassurance and comfort in the one they pledged their lives to. They separated once, then joined their mouths again, deepening the kiss for just a moment before Darcy pulled away. Brushing the backs of his fingers over her cheek, he whispered, "I adore you."

Elizabeth smiled at his words, returning his sentiments before laying her head back down on his shoulder. They remained embraced for a few more minutes, until steps could be heard on the staircase. Jane, who had led her sister out of the bedroom then disappeared back into it when her future brother embraced Elizabeth, stepped once again into the hall and cleared her throat.

Reluctantly, the couple separated, Darcy lifting Elizabeth off his lap and onto the seat next to him before rising. Nodding to Jane, he turned back to his intended, holding out his hand and helping her to rise. He escorted her down the stairs with Jane following.

Elizabeth did her best, after being settled into a chair with a blanket over her legs, to be her usual self, but the effort was exhausting. While the majority of the party, which this day included the Hursts, were encouraging and understanding of the trauma she had faced, Mrs. Bennet was her usual self. She often praised Darcy and Bingley, for various reasons but largely because they were marrying her girls. However, every time her eyes fell upon her second daughter, she would recall the near-ruin she had brought upon them by disappearing. As a result of these recollections, she berated Elizabeth as an undutiful and wild child who had no compassion on her poor nerves.

The words, combined with her mother's shrill voice and her own lingering weakness, were more than Elizabeth could take. She held on as long as she could, but her distress was clear to everyone who cared to see it. Darcy waited for Bennet to take control of his wife and when he did not, Darcy did.

Standing from his chair beside his betrothed, he apologized to the gathering. "I am sorry to interrupt, but Elizabeth is fatigued and requires rest. I will escort her to her room."

"Oh, Lizzy is well. All she wants is attention. You will have your hands full with her, Mr. Darcy."

Darcy's mien transitioned from blankly polite to menacing. He stiffened with the affront to his future wife and took a full minute to gather his control enough to speak. When he did, however, there was no doubt even in Mrs. Bennet's mind that he was greatly displeased with her.

"There is *nothing* wanting in Elizabeth, Mrs. Bennet. She is neither wild nor untamed. She is *not* uncaring. What she is, is recovering from a horrific experience that was *no fault of her own.* A scoundrel tried to use her to revenge himself on me. If you are going to blame anyone for your nerves being overset, you should be attributing them to me and my actions, *not* your daughter's.

"In addition, she is *not* well, and if you had eyes for anyone but yourself, you would see this. She almost died, Mrs. Bennet. Died! You should be *praising* her for her efforts to release herself from her bindings while in that building. You should be *praising* her for being out of bed after only a week of recovery. Your careless, thoughtless words have the potential to set her back again. The wedding would have to be postponed in that case. What do you say about that, Mrs. Bennet?"

Darcy's harsh words left the entire room silent, including Elizabeth's mother, who was unaccustomed to being reprimanded for her behavior. He felt Elizabeth take his hand. Inhaling deeply in an attempt to calm the shaking that came along with his rage, he turned to her and helped her to her feet. Without another word or look at anyone, he picked her up and carried her out of the room. Jane, Mary, and Georgiana quickly followed, eager to be of use to the couple.

After a long, awkward silence, Lady Watts spoke. "Well, that was heartfelt. If there was ever a doubt about that young man's love for Elizabeth, his words should have put it to rest."

Her sister's speech woke Mrs. Bennet out of her shocked stupor and once again loosened her tongue. "Why, I never! He had no right to speak to me that way! I can-"

"Yes, Wife, he did have the right. Shame on me for not stopping you myself. Your future son had the right of it. What happened to our daughter was not her doing, and I had best not hear you speak of it or her again in that manner. Mr. Darcy may just be the salvation from the hedgerows that you have been so afraid of for so long. I expect you to treat both him and Elizabeth with the proper respect. I intend to encourage them to marry as soon as possible. Darcy has the license in his possession; the marriage articles have been signed. All that is left is to stand in the church. They need each other far more than you and I will ever understand." With those words, Bennet bowed to the remaining guests and retreated to his book room.

Lady Watts waited until she heard the book room door close to speak in support of her brother. "Thomas was correct, Fanny. Elizabeth did not choose to be kidnapped and left to die. The man who did this was using her to hurt Darcy. She is fragile right now, physically and, I would imagine, in her emotions. By berating her on her first foray into the world since her recovery, you have made her ill again. You must learn to see things from another perspective than your own, Sister. I know you love all your girls; you must show it to all of them, even the ones you do not understand."

Silence ruled the room once again. Before the mistress of the house could regain her tongue after her third set down in a row, the Hursts excused themselves to return to Netherfield. They said not a word about it, not in the carriage or upon returning home, but both felt that it was long past time someone took Longbourn's mistress to task.

Mrs. Bennet, unable to think of a single thing to say to defend herself, rose and, without a word, retired to her rooms. She would spend the rest of the day there, taking meals on a tray and admitting no one to see her.

~~~***~~~

Having carried his beloved to her room, Darcy gently set her on the bed, sitting beside
~~~

her when she would not release him. Silently he held her while she cried once more into his shoulder and their sisters quietly busied themselves around the room. Finally, she calmed enough to speak.

"I do not know what to say first."

"There is nothing you need to say. I apologize for my part in your distress. I should not have let my temper loose as I did."

"All is well, my love. Mama deserved every word you spoke to her. Thank you for standing up for me."

Darcy kissed her softly. "I was happy to be your defender. You are my wife in my heart, and will officially be very soon. It is my duty and my pleasure to defend you against all attacks."

Elizabeth smiled gently, running her hand over his cheek, before looking down and speaking again. "I am sorry for my mother and her unchecked words. I am sorry you had to sit in that room and hear her go on." Elizabeth sighed. "Would that my father had done something with her long ago."

"You are not to blame, my love. Your mother has the power of choice just as you and I do. She has had proper examples all around her, both in her family and in her neighbors and friends, and yet she has still chosen to behave as she wished instead of properly."

"True." Elizabeth paused. "Still, I would rather you had not been exposed to her ridiculousness. I love her, I do, but I do not always like her. Does that make me a bad person?"

"Not at all. We must love our family, and usually do, but everyone has characteristics that cause us to turn away from them on occasion. We love our family, but we do not always have to like them."

Nodding, Elizabeth smiled at him. "How did you become so wise?"

Darcy chuckled, heartened to see her smiling and her good humor returning. "I do not know. Let us call it experience with my own ridiculous family members and leave it at that. Now, not to change the subject, but I can see the exhaustion in your face, my love. You need to let your sisters help you into a nightgown so you can rest. I will be on my settee in the hallway in case you need me."

"Very well. I will see you later. I see Mrs. Hill hovering, and you know how she frowns upon bad behavior. I love you."

Bestowing one last kiss to her upturned lips, Darcy rose. Bowing to each of the girls and the housekeeper, he exited the room.

"Mrs. Hill." Jane giggled. "You seem to have frightened Mr. Darcy."

"Well, one must keep these young men behaving properly, you know. If you give them an inch ..."

The girls laughed at the wink that accompanied the housekeeper's words. They set about undressing Elizabeth and soon had her tucked into bed and fast asleep.

In the hallway, Bennet approached Darcy, who rose and bowed before inviting him to sit.

"How is Elizabeth?"

"She was upset and crying, but we discussed it and I believe we both feel better." He looked Bennet in the eye. "She tried to take the blame for her mother's behavior. I assured her that Mrs. Bennet's actions were a result of her own choices, regardless of your neglectfulness of the situation."

Bennet looked to his hands in embarrassment. "Yes, well, I admit to taking amusement in her antics. I have not worried over my daughters' responses to them, or to my failure to stop them. I am ashamed to see that my deficiency has so affected my girls. I fear, though, that it is far too late to attempt to amend my wife's behavior."

Darcy eyed him for a moment before speaking. "That is between you and your other daughters. My concern is with Elizabeth. She is a gem, and you know it. How your wife could miss it is beyond my understanding, but I suspect Elizabeth has the right of it when she says that Mrs. Bennet used her beauty and liveliness to gain a husband and has no understanding of using her mind for such a thing. Regardless, she does not show care for her daughter, and I am of a mind to marry quickly to remove Elizabeth from her mother's censure."

Bennet sighed. "I had suspected you might. I know that everything is in place for you to wed. I will support you in this, and I have already told my wife so. Do you have a firm date?"

"I have not spoken to Elizabeth of it, but I should like to have the ceremony in three days' time. She should be recovered enough at that point to tolerate the half day's ride to town. We shall remain there for a few days and then go home to Pemberley."

"Very well, then. I will speak to the rector this afternoon." He stood. "Thank you for your care for Elizabeth. She has chosen well, and I know she will be happy with you."

Darcy also rose. "Thank you, sir. She is my life, and I would do anything for her."

<div align="center">~~~***~~~</div>

Three days later, Elizabeth and Darcy were wed in Longbourn's church in a joint ceremony with Jane and Bingley. Their joy at finally being united was clear to their audience, which included Darcy's sister and his cousin, Colonel Fitzwilliam, along with the Bennets, their relations, and most of Meryton.

At the wedding breakfast, as the newly married couples made their way around to greet each guest, the neighbors remarked on how quiet Longbourn's mistress was. Not one could recall a time when she had not crowed about her accomplishments, and surely having two daughters so well married was a great achievement. What they were not aware of was the confrontation between Darcy and his mother-in-law that had effectively silenced her while he remained in her home. Mr. Bennet had sworn the family to secrecy about it, and no one was brave enough to risk his unprecedented wrath.

As soon as they had a moment, Elizabeth and Darcy joined Jane and Bingley as they stood in front of the fireplace.

"Darcy, I owe you my thanks for encouraging me to purchase that special license. It means a great deal to Jane for us to be able to marry alongside you and Elizabeth."

"It was the least I could do. It was wise of you to begin the settlements while you were still in town. It only made sense to be prepared for anything."

"I imagine, Fitzwilliam," said Jane, "that you suspected you would require a quicker wedding than originally planned."

"Indeed, I did. It did not take me long to realize so, and when Elizabeth went missing, I swore that if she lived, I would marry her as soon as possible." He lifted his wife's hand from his arm and bestowed a tender kiss upon it as he stared deep into her eyes.

"What are your plans?" Bingley knew that if someone did not break their concentration, his friend and Elizabeth would stare at each other all day.

"We are to spend a week in London, are we not, my love?"

"Yes, Elizabeth is correct. A week in London and then off to Pemberley. I am eager to show it off to its mistress, and show the mistress off to Pemberley." He smiled at her blush. Looking to his friend, he asked about their plans.

"We are spending tonight in town, as well, at the Clarendon. The Hursts will stay here in Hertfordshire for a while and keep the house open for us. We plan a brief tour of the kingdom, and I wish to show Jane the town where I grew up and my father's mills."

"I am eager to meet the rest of Charles' family."

"You mean you wish to see if they are like me or like Caroline." Bingley laughed. He had told Jane the story of his younger sister and how she was found in Darcy's bed one night by a servant, who informed Mrs. Hurst, who took her husband, brother, and Darcy with her to confront her sister, exposing her and her machinations to the entire household.

Jane smiled without replying, but Darcy and Elizabeth chuckled at the thought, for Darcy had also told Elizabeth the story, leaving it to her to share the whole embarrassing incident with Georgiana.

They were interrupted in their laughter by Colonel Fitzwilliam, who had Darcy's sister with him. "Congratulations, Darcy, Mrs. Darcy. I wish you every happiness."

"Thank you, Cousin. Are you leaving?"

"Yes, I must return to my regiment tomorrow, so I thought to deliver Georgiana and Mrs. Annesley to their establishment and spend the night at my father's house. He will want a report of the day, you know."

"That, he will. Make sure he understands that if he wishes to retain a relationship with me, he must accept Elizabeth openly and publicly."

"I will."

"That other matter ..."

Colonel Fitzwilliam looked his cousin in the eye. "Has been taken care of. There was a robbery recently, late at night, in Seven Dials. Apparently, the victim tried to fight off the thief and was killed for his efforts. It is a mystery that will likely remain unsolved."

Darcy raised his brow. "I see." Nothing more of the matter was said by either gentleman.

By the time they finished speaking, Georgiana had completed her goodbyes to her new sisters and Mr. Bingley. She hugged her brother, whispering to him that she loved him and thanking him for giving her sisters, then turned to the door where Mary waited for her turn at leave-taking.

Less than an hour later, the Darcys also farewelled the gathering. They entered the coach, ready to begin their new life.

~~~***~~~

The man ran as fast as he could, ducking down dark alleys and deserted mews, trying to evade the man who chased him. This part of London was known for its crime, and one never knew what one might find. Most people, even those who lived in this neighborhood, refused to venture out at night.

He had thought for weeks that he was being followed, but had never been certain. There had been no more than a shadow that was there and then gone. He had not recognized faces, and after his actions in Hertfordshire, he knew it was imperative that he pay attention to such things. Tonight, though ... tonight there was a face he did know. And so he ran.

Suddenly, out of the murky London fog, as he came to the end of a building, a man in a red uniform stepped into his path. The running man slid to a halt, his heart in his throat.

"Wickham."

"F-fitzwilliam."

Colonel Fitzwilliam took a step forward, grabbing Wickham's cravat with one hand and pulling him closer. Snarling into his face, he spoke. "You abducted a gentlewoman and left her to die. What does that make you, hmm?"

"Uhh ..."

"That makes you an attempted murderer. What do they do to attempted murderers?"
~~~

When Wickham did not answer, the colonel shook him. "Answer me!"

"They ... they hang them."

"They do, and when you hang you die. You have committed your last crime. Goodbye, George." With a swift motion, he thrust a stiletto under Wickham's ribcage, twisting as he had been taught to do by the Frenchman who trained him to use the ancient weapon, before pulling it back out. He let go of Wickham's cravat and watched as he slumped to the ground. Rifling through the dying man's pockets, he tossed the contents around him before wiping the knife on Wickham's coat. Retracting the blade and then sliding the weapon back into the specially-made sheath in his boot, Fitzwilliam surveyed the scene one more time before slipping again into the dark shadows.

Before you go ...

If you enjoyed this book, please consider leaving a review at the store where you purchased it.

Also, consider joining my mailing list at https://mailchi.mp/ee42ccbc6409/zoeburtonsignup

~Zoe

About the Author

Zoe Burton first fell in love with Jane Austen's books in 2010, after seeing the 2005 version of Pride and Prejudice on television. While making her purchases of Miss Austen's novels, she discovered Jane Austen Fan Fiction; soon after that she found websites full of JAFF. Her life has never been the same. She began writing her own stories when she ran out of new ones to read.

Zoe lives in a 100-plus-year-old house in the snow-belt of Ohio with her Boxer, Jasper. She is a former Special Education Teacher, and has a passion for romance in general, *Pride and Prejudice* in particular, and stock car racing.

Connect with Zoe Burton

Email:

zoe@zoeburton.com

Facebook:

https://www.facebook.com/ZoeBurtonBooks

https://www.facebook.com/groups/BurtonsBabes/

Website:

https://zoeburton.com

Support me at Patreon:

https://www.patreon.com/zoeburtonauthor

Join my mailing list:

https://mailchi.mp/ee42ccbc6409/zoeburtonsignup

Pinterest:

https://www.pinterest.com/zoeburtonauthor

Darcy's Christmas Compromise

Darcy's Predicament

Darcy's Uneasy Betrothal

Darcy's Yuletide Wedding

Darcy's Unwanted Bride

Darcy's Favorite

Darcy's Christmas Scheme

Mr. Darcy: The Key to Her Heart

Darcy's Happy Compromise

Darcy's Honorable Proposal

Victorian Romance:

A MUCH Later Meeting

WESTERN ROMANCE:

Darcy's Bodie Mine